An Odd Soul

That night after my prayers I lay awake thinking about Forrest. I was torn. I was wildly attracted to him and equally terrified of him.

In one of my fairy stories, a dragon appeared when little Mary Ellen was in serious trouble. He was not a tame dragon but a wild one. He wasn't sure what he wanted to do with Mary Ellen – breathe fire on her, eat her for lunch, or let her ride on his back.

Forrest was like that dragon. He might burn me. He might eat me. Or he might take me on a delightfully magical journey.

In my fairy story, Mary Ellen made friends with the dragon and took that enchanted flight but that was a fairy story, not real life.

A Points to Ponder Book

Ozark Heritage Points to Ponder books are non-traditional stories sometimes incorporating elements of fantasy but reflecting Christian values and raising thought provoking ethical or moral questions.

Also by Mary Cambron-Collard

Family Secrets
Survivor's Guilt
Incident at Indian Cave
McDugal's Kirk: Book 1 of the Bigfoot Tales
Redemption: Book 2 of the Bigfoot Tales
Feud: Book 3 of the Bigfoot Tales

Coming Soon
Guilty
Searching: Book 4 of the Bigfoot Tales

E-mail: cambroncollard@gmail.com

OHP
OZARK HERITAGE PUBLISHING
723 North Ninth Street
Poplar Bluff, Missouri
E-mail: ozarkheritagepublishing@gmail.com

Printed by CreateSpace, An Amazon.com Company.

Dear Readers,

Many stories are conceived in ambiguity – points of confusion, things not quite understood, questions with several possible answers.

And the food that feeds those stories is imagination.

This is a tale of imagination, intuition, coincidences, Second Sight, or prophetic ability – any, all, or none of which may be true, or not true, depending on how the viewer sees it.

But welcome to the Davis General Store and Dragon Hold, located at Green Valley, somewhere on Highway 60 between Van Buren and Ellsinore, Missouri – or maybe existing only in our imaginations.

Come and meet "an odd soul."

Sincerely,
Mary Cambron-Collard

Email: cambroncollard@gmail.com

THANKS

My thanks for this story go out to all the people
at Country Bumpkins, Somewhere in Time,
and Maverick Glass
which all very much exist.
Also I salute the operator of the landing strip
at Four Corners who will remember
my father, Rev. Leonard Collard, the Circuit Rider,
and his 1948 Stinson aircraft.

An Odd Soul

Mary Cambron-Collard

OHP

Ozark Heritage Publishing

A Points to Ponder Book

This is a work of fiction. Any resemblance to actual persons, living or dead, is completely coincidental.

Copyright © 2017 Mary Cambron-Collard
All rights reserved.

ISBN-10: 1542823005
ISBN-13: 978-1542823005

Cover Photo: Klepzig Mill
by Diana Collard

Printed by CreateSpace, an Amazon.com Company

Though He slay me, yet will I trust in Him.
Job 13:15a (KJV)

Chapter 1: Sue Ellen

I inherited my Great Aunt Alice's ringed eyes and supposedly the Second Sight that went with them but at 20 years old, I knew if I truly had it, it was sporadic, and it certainly didn't seem to be working that day.

I was only driving 55 miles an hour on the four-lane divided highway posted 65 because I was trying to save gas. I had 37 dollars and 11 cents and I would have to buy gas again before I got to Cousin Marie's house. So when the dog ran out into the road, it had plenty of time to run on across. It stopped on the shoulder and looked at me, then turned its head to watch something else and I also looked. It was a child and she was running towards the dog. I hit my brakes and if she had kept running, it would have been fine, but she stumbled and fell right in the middle of my lane. I came to a screeching stop and knew I had not hit her but my rear-view mirror showed a large car barreling up behind me. I found the button for my flashers and prayed desperately.

The car swooshed past me in the other lane so fast, my old Ford Tempo rocked, and then I saw the car's brake lights go on. But with my rear-view mirror clear, I popped out of my car and ran around to the child. She was sitting up and crying and the dog was trying to comfort her. She was dressed in a small sleeveless shirt and shorts so her knees were skinned and bleeding. She looked maybe 3, going 4, and I said, "Honey, come to Dria," and held out my arms. She reached up and I scooped her up and moved to the shoulder of the highway.

The large car which had passed me had backed up and stopped on the shoulder. Now an older man jumped out and said, "How bad is she hurt?"

I looked at him and said, "Just skinned knees. I didn't actually hit her."

I heard the passenger side door of his car open and a well-kept looking middle-aged woman got out. She was on a cell phone and I knew instantly she had called 911. I said, "She isn't really hurt."

The woman closed her phone and said, "There's an ambulance on it's way."

Knowing the cost of ambulances, and their persistent insistence on getting paid, I said, "The child is not really hurt. Call and cancel the ambulance."

The woman said, "No. She should be checked by medical personnel."

I said, "I did not hit her. She just fell down while running across the highway chasing her dog. She isn't really hurt and since you called the ambulance, they will try to make you pay for it."

Her husband said, "Honey, call and cancel the ambulance. The child isn't even crying any more. If she was really hurt, she'd be crying."

The woman opened her phone and pushed the buttons and then passed the phone to her husband. "You talk to them," she said.

Another vehicle went by but didn't stop. I looked around. Just ahead of us was a turn-through on the divided highway for a side road going left. I could see a sign saying "Davis General Store." Past a hedge, on the left of the side road I could see the top part of a large two-storied rock building with dormer windows in the steeply pitched roof. On the right of the side road was a house.

As I put the child in my car I thought about the coincidence. My last name is Davis. When the dog whined, I let her in my car too, thinking she might be a comfort for the child. She was some sort of mid-sized shepherd, multi-colored, and she readily obeyed my command and sat in the floorboard with her head in the child's lap. As I fastened the child into a seat belt with my pillow, I asked her, "What's your dog's name?"

"Thpot," she said. "Thee'th Gwanny'th dog. Gwanny named her Thpot."

"Spot," I said, understanding her three-year-old lisp easily. "That's a nice name. And do you have a name?"

She giggled. "My name'th Thue Ellen."

"Sue Ellen," I repeated. "That's a nice name too." I climbed into the driver's seat and said, "Let's go find your granny."

But little Sue Ellen had given me a shock which had nothing to do with her running out in front of my car. She had ringed eyes. Mine are black around the edges with a vivid purple-blue and then a definite green next to the pupil. Sue Ellen's were blue on the outside with a ring of brown and then yellow next to the pupil. I knew that both of us would be designated *hazel* on official documents even though our eyes were not the same at all. But they were both definitely ringed.

I parked in a bare area beside the store, noting a young woman with short purple spikes for hair putting gas in a silver colored Grand Marquis. I thought it was an odd car for her to be driving and noticed the Missouri license plate had two groups of three letters and digits. One side said TEA which I found amusing. Probably her grandmother's car, I thought, as I carried Sue Ellen into the store. The dog acted familiar with the place and stopped at the door which was fitted with an old fashioned bell which jangled as we entered. A young man with sandy-red hair was standing watching out the window. He looked at me and then focused his blue eyes on the child. "Sue Ellen!" he cried, looking horrified, and rapidly moved toward us.

"Daddy," the child called, reaching out her arms to him.

He took her and said to me urgently, "What happened?"

"She ran out into the highway. I didn't hit her but she fell and skinned her knees." Unexpectedly, I found tears streaming down my face. I was embarrassed. "I'm sorry," I said. "It just scared me so bad." I started digging in my purse for a tissue. "We need to wash her knees," I said, "and put something on them." I wanted the focus off me.

He looked toward a curtained doorway at the back of the store behind the counter and said, "Granny was watching her."

He moved to go through the curtain and I followed him. On the other side past stairs going up was a large living room with elderly furniture but no granny. He crossed the room diagonally to a doorway calling, "Granny?" but there was no answer. I followed to find a kitchen and straight ahead a back door standing open. Through the screen door, a large backyard was visible and the man exclaimed, "Oh, no."

I followed him out the door and saw an elderly woman on the ground near a garden. She was trying to crawl toward the building. The man handed me Sue Ellen and ran.

Granny had fallen and hurt her ankle. The man helped her into the house, half carrying her. I heard her call him Glen. She was insisting it was only a sprain but he was worried that she had broken something. I said, "Let me check."

"Are you a nurse?" Glen asked.

"No," I told him, "a pre-school teacher. We have to take First Aid training and I just did one recently."

As I moved to look, we heard the store bell jangle and Glen hesitated but then went through the curtain. He was back quickly muttering, "Danged thieves. They gas up and if I'm not right on top of them, they drive off."

"Silver colored Grand Marquis?" I asked.

Glen looked at me sharply. "Yes," he said.

"Young woman with purple spiked hair. The license plate had the letters TEA."

While I poked and prodded on Granny's ankle, he made a call on his cell phone. When he hung up, I said to the elderly woman, "I do think it's only a sprain. Do you hurt anywhere else?"

"Well, when I fell, I hit my side on a rock but I think it's just a bruise."

I was careful. Old bones are fragile. When she took a deep breath, it provoked a sharp pain. I said, "You could easily have cracked a rib. You probably should have an x-ray."

I wrapped Granny's ankle and made ice packs. I washed Sue Ellen's knees and put antibiotic ointment on them while listening to Glen trying to persuade Granny to go for an x-ray. He ducked out twice to wait on customers. After another jangle, he came back with a large uniformed man wearing a Smokey style hat. He was holding a clipboard and he said, "Miss, what's you name?"

I hesitated but knew I had to give it. It probably would be okay. Why would someone in California be interested in a witness to a minor theft incident in Southern Missouri? "Dria Davis," I said. "Actually it's Alexandria Davis which is a bit of a mouthful."

"Do you have any ID?" he asked and I was glad I had not tried to lie.

I produced my driver's license and he said, "Alexandria Margaret Davis. That is a mouthful. Bakersfield, California. Miss Davis, what brings you to Missouri?"

"Visiting relatives," I said and stopped, not knowing what else to say. The Davis General Store people somewhere between Van Buren and Ellsinore were not my relatives. I was headed over to a place called Fisk that was out from Poplar Bluff. I was only an hour or so from my destination but Davis is a common name and I didn't expect these Davis's were any kin.

The man in the hat nodded and went on, "Mr. Davis here says you are the one who saw the woman who drove off and got a partial plate number."

I agreed. "I noticed because she didn't fit the car. She had her hair in short purple spikes and she had a lot of tattoos. She was wearing a purple tank top and black leggings with what looked like hiking boots. She was driving a silver Grand Marquis which is an old people's car. Then the license plate had TEA on it and I imagined her taking tea with an old lady who was her grandmother." I looked at the law officer with consternation. "I'm sorry," I told him, "but that's what went through my mind."

He had a slight frown and I told myself to keep my wayward thoughts to myself. Then he pulled a smart phone out of his shirt pocket and found a picture. "Is this the car?" he asked.

"Looks like it," I said. "Can you zoom in on the license plate?"

He did and I said, "Yes, that's the car."

He found another photo. "And this woman?" he asked.

"Yes." I said instantly.

"You're sure?"

"Yes, I remember the belt she's wearing also." I decided not to add it was a type gang members used for fighting. A young woman might use one for defense as well.

He nodded and put the phone away and started writing on his clipboard again. He said to me, "If Mr. Davis presses charges and it goes to court, he'll need you for a witness."

I started to explain that I might not be here but he said, "Now what's this about a child being out on the highway?"

With Granny obviously incapacitated and her dress torn and dirty from trying to crawl, it was not difficult to persuade the officer that Sue Ellen's adventure was a one time occurrence, not an on-going case of child neglect.

His commented, "That call about the child is why we had several cars out here and caught your gas thief." Granny asked if he wanted to sit at the kitchen table and have some iced tea while he filled out his report. The bell on the store door jangled again and Glen went to answer it.

As the officer moved to the dining table, Granny motioned for me to lean down and she said softly, "Let's let that officer think you're family. It's looks better that way. Glen and his wife had a big dust-up yesterday and she left. She may not come back and we don't want the gossips saying he's got another woman in here already."

I had never in my short – and until recently, very quiet – life been cast as the *Other Woman*. I was amused.

Granny directed me to give Sue Ellen milk and cookies so I tried to act like I lived here while I served iced tea, milk, and cookies.

The officer's phone buzzed and after a short conversation, he hung up and said, "Miss, do you by any chance have some kind of Second Sight?"

I was jolted and couldn't think of a thing to say but he was grinning. "That girl stole that car from her grandmother. She had coffee with her grandmother and they think she gave the old lady a sleeping pill. When the grandmother woke up, she found the girl, the car, her money, her check book, and her credit cards all gone."

The officer finished his paperwork and his iced tea. He told Sue Ellen to stay out of the highway and left. By that time, Granny was drooping and she agreed to let Glen take her for an x-ray. More customers had been coming and going from the store and they asked me rather diffidently if I could possibly stay and deal with customers. They had a sign which they put out when they were closed saying if it was urgent, to ring the bell and someone would come.

Granny said, "It's a ways into town and sometimes people really need something. If we aren't accommodating, we lose customers and we need them. Besides, you need to change your clothes. There's a washer and detergent in the bathroom." I saw that taking care of the store would encourage Granny to let Glen take her for an x-ray so I agreed and Glen fetched a bag out of my car for me.

It was Granny who asked diffidently if they could leave Sue Ellen with me. I had thought of suggesting it but they didn't really know me. However, Glen did not need to be trying to handle a fussy 3-year-old up past her bedtime along with an injured grandmother. Glen gave me quick run-down on things. A customer arrived for the store and I let Sue Ellen push keys on the cash register while Glen and Granny left, thus avoiding the possibility of a scene with a crying child being left behind.

As soon as the customer was gone, I poured out a bag of Mega Blocks and started building something. It didn't take long for Sue Ellen to insist on building something herself.

I started scrubbing the blood stains out of the blouse I had been wearing and another customer came who clearly was a regular. He said, "I'm glad you're here. My wife phoned me to stop for milk."

I finished washing my blouse and hung it out on the clothes line near the back door.

I was unsure what to do next. I was on my way to my grandmother's cousin. It was only an hour or so from where I now was on Highway 60 east of Van Buren. When I had called, I had only talked to her daughter. The daughter had not been enthusiastic about my visit and I was hoping her mother would be more welcoming.

I was looking for a place to hide.

My father had died almost six months ago. He was a lawyer and he was killed in a courtroom where he had been representing a mother in a child custody dispute. The father of the child had shot my father and his ex-wife but missed the judge. My father died but the ex-wife lived. The shooter was now out on bail. Some things just don't make sense.

And others make too much sense. Next April, when I will turn 21, I am slated to inherit some money, quite a lot of money actually. My step-mother, Belle, wants it.

When my father made his Will, he had named three trustees in case he died before I turned 21. In spite of being a lawyer, he had not updated his Will when one of those three trustees died. That left two.

My step-mother, Belle, had gotten one of them into her pocket, or more explicitly, her bed. The other one was on a sabbatical in Europe. Belle's cohort could not really do anything without the other trustee's okay and so far, he seemed willing to listen to me but communication with him was erratic.

So my step-mother had set a trap. I came home from work and found Bell preparing to go out. She told me she had left my dinner in the kitchen. I went straight up to my room, planning to eat after she was gone.

When I opened the door to my room, I smelled her perfume. She had been in my room. I began looking for why.

I found the bottle of prescription pills hidden in my underwear drawer. They were strong painkillers, Oxycontin. I knew immediately her plan was to accuse me of stealing them. I took the bottle to her room and quickly found paper and wrote a note saying, "It didn't work."

I knew when this plot failed, she would think of another one. Belle was inheriting the house and I was already planning to move, even though I had the right to live here until I was 21. Now I quickly packed some clothes and carted bags and boxes down to my car. My car was an ancient Ford Tempo but it only had about 48,000 miles on it and Dad had taken good care of it. So far, it had been totally reliable. When the trunk and the back seat were full, I went to the kitchen and saw Belle had left me a nice meal including cheese and broccoli soup which she knew I adored. Such thoughtfulness was so unlike Belle, I immediately became suspicious. It occurred to me she might have put some of the Oxycontin in my food and intended for me to be caught with drugs in my system.

I put the food in a box and sat it in the passenger seat of my car. On my way to the police station, I stopped at an ATM. I discovered my card would only give me two hundred dollars. It was too late for me to go to my bank for more.

At the police station, I explained I was sure my step-mother was trying to drug me. I wanted the food tested for Oxycontin. I was put in a small room and eventually a lady police officer came to talk to me. I slowly realized she thought I was either some kind of mental case or was trying to get back at my step-mother for something. When there came a knock on the door, she went out of the room. I got up and cracked the door. Another police officer was saying, " . . . there's a history of problems. She said she'd come down to the station and pick her up."

I knew they had called Belle. The lady police officer went down the hall to a restroom and I slipped out. My heart was pounding but I walked at a normal pace without looking around. Outside I climbed into my car and left Bakersfield headed east on Highway 58. I bought gas in Barstow, paying cash. I didn't want to leave a trail. Somewhere on I-40 out in the Mojave Desert, I found a Rest Area and I rearranged my stuff so I could lean a seat back and sleep in a semi-comfortable position.

By morning, I had a plan. I turned around and returned to Barstow but stayed on I-40 and went to the Los Angeles Complex. Somewhere in Pasadena, I got off and found a library. I located a branch of my bank and withdrew money. I left 5 dollars in my account which meant I had about 800 dollars in cash. I had just been paid or there would not have been that much. I knew my step-mother would find out where I withdrew the money. She would think of some reason for the bank to tell her.

I went back to the library I had found and started trying to find Grandmother's cousin. She had come when my mother died. I was 10 but Mama had really been gone since I was 4. She had been pregnant and slipped on a muddy spot on a sidewalk and fell. She lost the baby but even worse, she suffered a serious head injury which left her in a nursing home unable to walk or talk. I did have a some memories of her from before the accident and Grandmother helped me to remember but her death was less of an event than her accident years before.

Grandmother's Cousin Marie had come for Mama's funeral and

stayed a few days. She had looked at me and said to Grandmother, "She's got your sister's ringed eyes. Does she have the Sight?"

It was the first I heard about the Sight but by the time I was 12, I knew I sometimes had ideas about things I logically could not know. However, it was sporadic and often not about anything important. Today's incident of thinking maybe the girl with purple hair was driving her grandmother's car was typical. It could have just been a guess.

The day Dad was killed, I had not anticipated anything.

I was thinking about all this when the store bell rang again. I picked up Sue Ellen and went to see who wanted what. It was an older woman and when I opened the door, she demanded to know who I was.

Mindful of Granny's injunction to let people think I was a relative, I said, "Dria Davis. Granny sprained her ankle and I'm babysitting Sue Ellen while Glen is taking her to the doctor."

"I live over there," she said, indicating the house across the side road. "I saw that child out in the road. I came over to see if that policeman took her away. I called that hot-line number for child abuse."

I looked at the woman in disbelief. I finally said, "You saw Sue Ellen out in the road?"

"Sure did," the woman said. "She was playing around out by the highway with her dog and no adult in sight."

"You saw her out alone and you didn't go get her?" I asked.

"She's not my grandkid," the woman said, "and I'm not her babysitter."

I exploded. This woman had watched a three-year-old playing alone by a high speed highway in front of her house and did nothing about it. She had even known who the child was. I was angry and I didn't hold back. "Lady," I said, "you are guilty of child endangerment. You saw a child in danger and did nothing about it. My father was a lawyer and I know what the law says. You can be prosecuted for criminal child endangerment." I was making up terms now. I didn't know what the charge was called but I knew that anyone who saw a child in danger and did nothing was guilty of something.

The woman moved, somehow puffing herself up bigger. "I'll have you know I'm a good Christian woman," she stated, "and I don't let my grandkids run loose in the road."

I was furious. "No you're not," I said fiercely. "You're a hypocrite."

I slammed the door and found that I was in tears. Sue Ellen started crying. I pushed the woman out of my mind and comforted Sue Ellen, feeling contrite because my anger had upset her.

I noticed the store and living quarters behind it were really only half of the large building. It had front and back porches going all the way across and I went out on the the back porch and looked through the windows on the other side. I saw a huge old kitchen and past that on the corner of the building, a room with a counter and furniture stacked and covered with dust sheets. I walked down the other side of the the building to the front porch. I saw a lot of bare space and furniture covered with dust sheets at the back of a large room. Also at the back of the room, was a staircase matching the one in the living quarters behind the store only this one had been left open on the front side. The building also had two external staircases on each side at the back. In case of fire maybe?

As I was looking, another car arrived and in the next couple of hours more than a dozen customers appeared. Mostly they wanted milk, baby formula, or diapers, things like that. A man wanted gas and I had to tell him that I didn't know how to turn on the pump. He did, so I sold him gas.

One customer was a little strange. I had heard her drive up to the gas pump and watched her discover it was turned off. She was wearing camo but looked pretty normal so I opened the door with no reservations. She looked surprised and said, "Who are you?"

Since that was exactly how the neighbor across the road started, I was immediately tense but I answered her exactly the same way. She responded with, "Where's Pam?"

Guessing that Pam might be Glen's wife but not being sure, I answered, "I don't know."

"She's supposed to be here," the woman complained. "When will she be back?"

"I'm not sure," I said. "If you'd like to leave a note, I'll pass it on."

"Just tell her to call Barb, okay?" was her answer and she turned away.

"Do you want gas?" I called out but she said no and drove off. I thought it a bit odd that she had tried to pump gas but then refused it when I offered.

I fixed Sue Ellen a scrambled egg with cheese and toast for supper. She needed a bath but bathing someone else's child with no one around might leave me open to misconduct allegations so I put her to bed dirty.

Between the store and the living quarters was a stairway that I thought led up to bedrooms but off the living room was a bedroom with twin beds and a crib. When I asked Sue Ellen if she wanted to sleep there, she said, "Nap time," and I guessed it probably was her usual napping spot. When she was settled with a green stuffed dragon she called Puff, she pointed to a boom box on the top of a dresser and said, "Muthic." I checked and found a CD in it. It was an old Peter, Paul, and Mary album which included "Puff the Magic Dragon."

I made myself scrambled eggs and toast and wondered where I was going to spend the night. I had been sleeping in my car and I could do that again but I wanted it parked in a safe, well-lit place.

Glen didn't come home until about 10 with Granny. He had her in a wheelchair. They had been to a clinic up in Ellington. The x-ray had revealed one broken rib and two others cracked. They had her ankle professionally wrapped and had given her a prescription for pain.

Granny had arrangements sorted out in her mind. She and I would sleep in the downstairs bedroom with Sue Ellen. Glen slept upstairs. They had me move my car around back into a berth in a long wooden building at the rear of the backyard. It had four open-fronted bays, each big enough for a car. The other end of the building was enclosed. Glen said, "This is the old carriage house and stables. It was built back before cars were common. There used to be a hotel and restaurant here."

While we were outside garaging my car and getting another bag, I told him about the woman who left a message for Pam. Glen looked a bit grim. I didn't want to tell him about the neighbor across the road but decided I had better. I told him what happened and apologized for getting mad. He huffed and said, "Mean spirited old hypocrite is exactly what she is. That woman is always gossiping and causing trouble. If there is anything that shouldn't be told, you can count on her to tell it!"

I said, "I was really angry. What kind of person sees a small child playing alone by a high speed highway and doesn't do anything about it? I am sure she can be charged with something."

Glen said, "Probably, but I would need a lawyer and I can't afford one." I saw the depressed look on his face. He and his wife were having trouble and divorces are expensive. And I knew already that he would want custody of Sue Ellen. His wife had left her with him but when it went to court, my experience was she would fight it just for spite.

Glen carried in the bag I wanted and then excused himself and went upstairs, saying he was exhausted.

I had a lovely bath in a huge old-fashioned footed tub and crawled into bed. I started praying but fell asleep before I got very far.

Chapter 2: Accusations

The next morning early, I heard Glen coming down the stairs. The noise woke Granny as well and I helped her get up and dress. She kept apologizing and I told her I normally helped small children and it wasn't much different. Sue Ellen woke up and I gave her cereal at the kitchen table. They opened the store at 7 every morning but Sunday.

Granny told Glen where to find a walker. She used it to move to the kitchen but she said her side hurt. I told her to just sit and tell me what to do.

At the breakfast table, she started asking me about my relatives. She was trying to figure out if her late husband and I were related but after 30 minutes, reluctantly concluded that we weren't. However, she said, "We are all descended from Adam so that makes us all distant kin."

She started asking me other things and I told her about my father dying and my step-mother trying to get what I was supposed to inherit. I didn't tell her what a large amount it was. Dad had disliked being ostentatious. I told her about the hidden pills and my realization while sitting in the police station that all my step-mother had to say was that I had put drugs in the food myself in order to get her in trouble. Police deal with rebellious children all the time and they tend to believe the parents.

We talked about my work as a pre-school teacher at a daycare center at my church. I had felt bad about calling and quitting with no advance notice. I hoped they would be willing to give me a good reference because I needed to find a job.

I told Granny about the fan belt on my car breaking somewhere in Arizona between Kingman and Seligman. The repair man had said he thought it was sabotage. I had bought gas in Kingman and came out of the restroom to find a man under the hood of my car "checking the oil." He had said my fan belts were old and I should replace them. I knew instantly he was lying but it was another one of those times when I wished my supposed Sight was more consistent. The bill for the tow truck and new fan belt had cost me most of my cash so I needed to go to work soon.

I had a credit card but I knew if I used it, Belle would find out where I had gone. It was a last resort.

I washed the few dishes and was planning to continue my journey when Granny asked me to send Glen to talk to her and would I mind keeping an eye on the store for a few minutes? The result of this was Glen and Granny asking if I would be willing to stay and help out for a few days. With Pam gone and Granny incapacitated, they really needed help. They offered room and board and ten dollars a day. Glen said, "I know it isn't much but the store hasn't been doing well."

I accepted the offer but explained that since I was trying to hide from my step-mother, would they mind if everyone thought I was related somehow? Granny said, "It's better if people think that. Like I told you, we don't want people saying Glen's got another woman already."

I called Grandmother's cousin's daughter and could tell she was relieved I wasn't coming. I told her I had already found a job up near Ellsinore but it was only temporary. She invited me to visit when I had a day off.

I asked about taking Sue Ellen outside and Granny had me help her into the wheel chair and roll her outside and park her under a large oak tree beside a picnic table. The back porch had a ramp on the unused side of the building and I saw another one going up to the front porch. I was officially introduced to the dog, Spot, who seemed well-behaved and Granny said she was unless she saw a rabbit or a squirrel to chase.

The backyard was bordered on the north by woods, on the south by the hedge which separated them from the highway, and at the back by the old carriage house which had more woods behind it. Under trees were two swings and a see-saw as well as a picnic table. Near the back porch was a small pump house with a water tap beside it. Back near the carriage house was an old pit toilet. In the center of the sheltered yard was a large kitchen garden.

Granny and I started talking about her garden. She had been working in the garden picking tomatoes when Spot started chasing a rabbit and Sue Ellen had taken off after the dog. She had tried to run after her and fell. She asked if I minded picking up the tomatoes she had dropped yesterday. I asked her for instructions and started working in the garden. Granny had bought some child sized garden tools for Sue Ellen to use and we had fun even if we weren't very efficient garden workers.

Besides Spot, they had some cats. Granny called one of them Lady and had me let her into the house. Granny said, "She's a real lady. She does her business outside and she never tears anything up and she's a good mouser."

We had sandwiches for lunch and afterwards, I gave Sue Ellen a bath before she went down for her nap. Granny was crocheting an afghan. I asked about internet and I was at the counter in the store trying to program Glen's WiFi password into my laptop when two men came into the store. Instead of shopping, one of them asked, "Glen, can I talk to you outside?"

Glen moved toward the door saying, "Sure, Ray. What's up?" Ray was a good-looking man with thick blonde hair, blue eyes, and handsome face features. The man with him was very tall with dark hair – a full beard and a braid down his back. I really didn't get a look at him before he turned and followed Glen and Ray outside but what I did see was that he was carrying a gun in a holster on his hip.

It jumped into my mind that Ray was angry about something although he had been smiling and hadn't sounded angry. I started for the door, watching as the three men went through and Ray turned toward Glen. He hit Glen in the face with his fist, sending Glen flying into a bench on the front porch of the store.

The door was only a screen-door and as I moved to open it, I heard Glen saying something. Ray answered him, "You beat my sister. Let's see if you can do the same to me!"

Glen was still sitting on the floor of the porch with blood running from his nose. He said, "I did not beat Pam. You should know better than to believe what your sister tells you."

"Pam called last night from the hospital emergency room and said you beat her."

"Pam left day before yesterday and I haven't seen her since. We caught her stealing and I banned her from the store," Glen said. "She's been stealing ever since we came up here. She's also been letting her friends steal things and gas too. Lately the store has not even been breaking even."

From the open door, I asked. "Glen, do you want me to call someone?"

Ray's head whipped around to look at me. "Who the hell are you?" he demanded.

"Dria Davis," I said, thinking this question was getting old. "Granny sprained her ankle yesterday and I'm here to help with Sue Ellen and Granny. If Glen beat anyone, it didn't happen last night."

Ray ripped out with a crudity and turned back to Glen saying, "Somebody sure beat her. She says it was you!"

"Well, it wasn't!" Glen said.

Then the tall, dark, bearded man with the gun turned to me and asked, "Was he here all last night?"

I moved through the door saying, "He took Granny to the doctor up in Ellington and they didn't get back until about 10. It was almost midnight by the time we got to bed. I was sleeping in that downstairs bedroom at the back and if Glen had left during the night, I would have heard the car."

The man nodded and it was only then that I saw his eyes. He had ringed eyes, exactly the same as Sue Ellen's, blue, brown, yellow. I felt confused, then it occurred to me that he must also be a relative. He had to be. Maybe Sue Ellen's mother also had the ringed eyes – or brown eyes which could be covering the hazel coloring. She couldn't be blue eyed like her brother, Ray. Glen's eyes were a clear light blue and two blue eyed people could not have produced Sue Ellen.

The two men left and Glen was holding a hanky over his nose. He said, "I'm probably going to get a black eye out of this. I'm glad Sue Ellen wasn't here. She's a sensitive little thing."

I dealt with a customer while Glen dealt with his nose and changed his shirt. Their cash register was a beautiful antique brass affair with elaborate decorations where they rang up total bills and deposited the payments. They had an adding machine for making receipts but it meant knowing tax rates which in Missouri vary for food and non-food. Glen had a helpful list of what was charged the higher non-food rate.

When Glen returned, I said, "I'm surprised you trust me to handle money. You don't really know me."

He shrugged. "When Granny told me Pam was stealing, I didn't want to believe it. We set a trap and it was real clear. Granny says she knew from the beginning that we shouldn't trust her but as long as the thievery was minor, she wasn't going to say anything. But when Pam started letting her friends carry stuff out, it got serious, especially the gas." He sighed and then said, "Granny says we can trust you. She was right about Pam and I expect she's right about you."

We got my computer connected to the internet and I e-mailed my trustee who was currently somewhere in Spain. Sometimes he would answer right away but other times it took several days so I wrote him a long e-mail telling him everything which had happened. However, I did not tell him where I was, only that I had a temporary live-in job taking care of an old lady and a three-year-old child.

I cooked a simple supper following Granny's directions. Before she died, Grandmother had been teaching me to cook but at 12, I hadn't gotten very far, and after she died Dad hired a housekeeper who cooked until he married Belle. With Belle, we either ate out or heated up things from cans or the freezer.

After Sue Ellen had her bath and went to bed, I discovered Granny and Glen were still keeping books using an old-fashioned ledger. Since Glen had a computer, I was surprised. He said he had been meaning to look into bookkeeping programs but hadn't had time. He was a school teacher and school had only just dismissed for summer a week ago. He had been teaching in Poplar Bluff which involved a commute and Granny had been slow to draw his attention to Pam's thieving because she needed Pam's help and she didn't want to upset Glen.

I was on my computer using the word processing program to add to my journal. I had helped at my father's office with the bookkeeping and I knew what program they had used but I told Glen he could probably find one designed for businesses like his. Granny started asking about computers and the internet and we talked peacefully until bed time. I returned my computer to the trunk of my car. I wanted it out of Sue Ellen's reach and that was easiest.

It was only when I was helping Granny to bed that I thought to ask about the man who had been with Ray. "Forrest Hunter," Granny told me. "He's an odd soul."

It was an intriguing remark and I wanted to know more but after finding out about Pam, I didn't want to ask awkward questions. While I hesitated, Granny sighed and went on. "I've always liked him but some around here thinks he's crazy. He's into all this survivalist stuff. He has published a couple of books about it. He owns a lot of land and every once in a while he has these Survival Training Courses, he calls them. He used to teach school but about five years ago, his wife and son were caught in a shooting over at Springfield. The boy was killed instantly and his wife was in a coma for more than two years before she died too. Forrest quit his teaching job and sat at the hospital with her a lot. When he wasn't at the hospital he was mostly drunk. After she died, he pulled himself together and started this survival training stuff. Sometimes he takes in a boy with problems and tries to help him. I think that's why he was with Ray. Ray has been in jail for stealing and only just got out. I think Forrest Hunter is trying to help him. Forrest is basically a good man but he needs to turn his troubles over to Jesus."

I smiled. She sounded just like my grandmother. It might seem like a simplistic solution but I had seen things happen in response to prayer and I was a Believer even though I had questions about how God worked – or sometimes didn't.

Granny directed me to a bookshelf in the living room and I came back with two books. Granny sold them in the store. These two were signed by the author. I saw that he was officially J. Forrest Hunter. Granny told me the J was for James. His father was James Hunter.

I finally asked what I wanted to know. "How is this Forrest Hunter related?"

Granny was suddenly still and then said, "Related? He's not related to us." I caught something in her voice, some under-note of tension.

"Oh," I remarked. "I thought he was some kin to Ray and that's why he was trying to help him." I didn't want to ask point blank about his eyes matching Sue Ellen's.

"No," Granny said. "Ray's people live in the Greenville area. Forrest Hunter's family are from over at Van Buren."

I was checking out one of the books and said, "Some of this looks interesting. 'How to Smoke Meat.' That might be useful to know."

Granny and I settled down to our individual prayers. Later in bed I thought about those ringed eyes again. Granny knew why Sue Ellen had Forrest Hunter's eyes but she wasn't going to talk about it. Secrets of that kind usually meant an illegitimate baby somewhere. Glen gave every evidence of loving Sue Ellen. If she wasn't his, I thought he would probably know. Pam must be related to Forrest Hunter in some way Granny didn't want to talk about.

As I waited for sleep to come, I thought about my grandmother. She had died the summer I was 12 and my life changed dramatically.

She had appendicitis. She had never been sick much and no one expected this to be fatal but there was some kind of complication with the anesthetic and she died during the operation. When they took her to the hospital, I had a vision of her in a casket and I told my father I thought she was going to die. He didn't want to hear it and I didn't insist. I still felt guilty and wondered if anything could been have done to prevent her death.

My father and I were both lost without Grandmother. I wrote my first serious poem, made a sketch of Grandmother which Dad framed, and I read a lot. My father met a woman named Belle Abernathy who was sympathetic and understanding.

I saw Belle briefly a dozen or so times and then Dad planned a day for the three of us at Disneyland. That evening at home, Dad said, "Well, honey, how did you like Belle?"

I said, "I'm sorry, Dad, but I really don't like her much." She had been sugar sweet all day but I knew it was an act.

He looked very disappointed and said, "She said that you'd be jealous."

I shook my head and said, "I'm not jealous. I wouldn't mind at all to have a new mom but I don't like her."

"Why not?" Dad asked.

"She's not who she pretends to be." Dad didn't take it seriously and two weeks later she talked Dad into going to Las Vegas and getting married.

At Belle's insistence, we moved from the roomy apartment over my father's law office in downtown Bakersfield to a new house out near Cal State. Over time, he began spending more and more time at his office and I found solace in my sketching and writing.

I had a friend with an imagination as active as mine named Regina whom Belle particularly disliked. She wanted me to make friends with the children of important people. Regina was fat and came from a large Catholic family. The church paid her school fees. I attended the Catholic school but we were Baptist. Belle was rude to Regina so we started going to Dad's office after school. And we started going over to Regina's house instead of her coming to mine. The first time I went, she was embarrassed but I told her where we used to live and her family was nice while my step-mother was mean.

To get to Dad's office and Regina's house, we took the city bus. She had a bus pass and I soon bought one too. The baptist church that I attended had a Wednesday evening program for teenagers. Regina started going with me.

Belle was interested in making the right friends, joining the right clubs, attending parties and social events, being seen in the right social circles. She insisted on Dad going with her but he hated it. Dad never said it but I knew he was not happy.

Then I was turning 16 and Dad sent me for driving lessons. He was giving me his old Ford Tempo. Belle had insisted on driving a BMW and was pressuring him to drive one too. She said his old car made him look like an eccentric.

Belle was having a big party for my sixteenth birthday but she was inviting her friends, not mine. It was a perfect example of her sugar sweet surface hiding a tartly sour inside. I wanted to invite my classmates at school and my baptist youth group but I realized it would be too awkward. Regina did not want to come but did because I wanted her. One of Dad's staff, a middle-aged widow, came and she rescued Regina. I wanted to sit with them but Belle kept pulling me away. She had invited several people with sons and daughters with whom she wanted me to form friendships. The boys looked at me with interest and one of them got me backed me into a corner and tried to kiss me. I kept going back to Regina and the widow. Belle kept trying to get me away from them. Finally one girl noticed and said, "What is with that woman?" I got her to join Regina and me with our older friend. She recruited her brother who recruited another boy and Belle finally left me alone. From the girl, her brother and his friend, I learned that Belle was not particularly well-liked by some of the people at the party.

With the freedom of my own car, I saw little of Belle. I knew she found me a disappointment and I didn't care. I knew my father had found her a disappointment and about that, I did care. I spent more time at his office and over at Regina's. Then that summer, the baptist church I attended was hiring teenage girls to help regular staff with daycare. With school out, working parents needed some place for their children. Regina and I were both hired and then again the next summer. The summer we graduated from High School, we also worked but Regina was gone for three weeks on a missions trip with a group from the Catholic church. They went to Calcutta, India to work in Mother Teresa's orphanage.

That fall, I started classes at Bakersfield Community Collage and Regina returned to Calcutta to join Mother's Teresa's ministry. She was still in Calcutta and happy. I started working on a pre-school teacher's certificate while working part-time at the church daycare. When I got the certificate, I became full-time and loved it.

Chapter 3: Retaliation

The next day was Saturday. Glen was developing a lovely purple, green, and yellow shiner. Granny had Glen rig a chair for her at the cash register so she could take money. She was working on an afghan between customers. Glen stocked shelves and Sue Ellen and I helped him. Sue Ellen loved it and I saw Glen was a good father. He talked to Sue Ellen and enjoyed her 3-year-old prattle.

We soon finished because the store did not carry that much stock. Besides food, it had an intriguing section of assorted hardware. It included kerosene lanterns and a good assortment of hand tools, nails, screws, and even can openers. They sold staples like flour, sugar, dry beans, cornmeal, salt, pasta, cooking oil, and shortening. They had a small rack of bread, chips, and snack cakes. Their canned goods were limited to basic stuff with an emphasis on easy to prepare items. They regularly got campers so they had camping supplies. They had two kinds of baby formula, a few bottles, and a fair stock of disposable diapers. They had bags of potatoes and onions. Granny's large garden produced more than they ate so the extra produce was sold in the store. They had a meat case with scales and a meat slicer behind it for slicing the assorted selection of meats and cheeses. They sold sandwiches and I had learned already they were a very popular item. In a refrigerated case, they had dairy products, canned biscuits, juices and cold drinks. The lowest shelf was empty. Beside the refrigerated case was a small chest type freezer with ice cream and a small selection of frozen foods including pizza, hamburger, and chicken. It was nearly empty and Glen told me he needed to go into Poplar Bluff that afternoon and get more supplies. When school had been in session, he had brought supplies every day. In the past, they had bought from wholesalers who delivered but the store's orders were so small, they now charged too much. Only the bread truck stopped three days a week. Hauling their own supplies was more economical.

Then Granny suggested she and I make the run to Poplar Bluff and take Sue Ellen. She said, "If Dria sees where we go and what we get, she can go in the future." I wondered how long Granny thought I was going to be here.

We took Glen's SUV and it turned out to be fun. With Granny using the wheelchair and me towing Sue Ellen, everyone was quick to offer help loading. Glen had sent coolers for refrigerated and frozen items and we arranged to pick them up last. Some things surprised me. Granny bought 20 yards each of two different fabrics in Walmart, one a navy blue and one a rust brown. Someone asked Granny who I was and she said, "Distant cousin helping us out while I can't get around."

On the way home, Sue Ellen fell asleep. Granny chatted. Her husband had died in March of pneumonia. Glen and Pam had moved up to help her run the store. She told me, "I was thinking about just closing it but my social security wouldn't be much and I've got some customers who depend on me. Some of them really can't get into town easily. Glen has been a big help. He's had some good ideas. This hauling stuff ourselves lets us offer better prices and more variety so sales are up."

Back at the store, Glen told Granny, "Your friend, Vergie, came in with one of her granddaughters. She had heard about you spraining your ankle. She said if she could be of any help, to let her know."

Granny laughed. "She's about old enough to be my mother and she can't see to drive anymore. If I needed a dulcimer player, she'd be real useful but I can't think of anything else she can do."

I put Sue Ellen in her crib and she didn't wake up. Granny said, "I'm going to have a little rest. You go help Glen and I'll let you know when Sue Ellen wakes up." We had found a bell for Granny to ring when she needed one of us.

Glen had unloaded the SUV. He carried most of the boxes inside but he had left a small pile of things on the bench on the porch, including the two pieces of fabric. I asked if he wanted them inside and he said, "No, that's a special order. We have some old style Amish living back beyond Green Valley who give us orders for certain things when we go into town. Their neighbor, Eb Smith, came in this morning and he said he'd give them a signal that they had stuff here."

A few customers came in after items like bread, milk, and sandwiches. Then a man came in who examined the refrigerated case and then looked around. "Where's the beer?" he asked.

"Sorry," Glen informed him, "we don't sell beer."

"How in the world do you keep this place going if you don't sell beer?" The man was clearly shocked.

Glen grinned. "This store has been here for more than a hundred years. We have a few loyal customers."

Then the man spied the can openers and said, "We need one of these." He started looking over the hardware and I heard something and looked outside. A horse and buggy arrived followed by a wagon pulled by two horses. The buggy had women and children and the women came inside while the children ran around the side of the building.

I heard Granny's bell and found Sue Ellen awake and wanting to join the children outside. I helped Granny into the wheelchair and took Sue Ellen outside. It wasn't long before a young man came around the building and said, "Miss, you can go join the women. I'll keep an eye on the young'uns."

I said, "If you need me, just come to the back door. I'm Dria Davis. I'm helping out while Granny's recovering."

The young man said, "I'm Samuel Miller." He was blushing and I realized that in spite of being above 6 feet in height, he was younger than me.

I found Granny in the living room with the three women drinking Kool-Aid. They had two babies and as I looked at them, I saw they must be twins, boys, nine or ten months old. A play pen had appeared from somewhere and Granny had given them Sue Ellen's Mega Blocks. They looked happy, one of them chewing on a block and the other walking around the edge of the play pen, holding on to the rail.

Granny introduced me to the women who were all named Miller. The two older women were Mary and Sarah while the younger woman was Elizabeth. The babies were hers and I asked how old they were. We chatted a while. They quilted and sent the quilts over somewhere near Rogersville to sell. Granny asked if they would like for her to try and sell them here. In the past, the store had sold all kinds of things they no longer handled like clothes and shoes. Granny said, "In the summer, we get tourists and they would buy quilts and handcrafts." Eventually a man stuck his head through the curtain to the store and said something which wasn't in English. It sounded like German and something about the young'uns. I guessed they were ready to go.

When they were gone, Granny told me the Amish had only been here a couple of years. They came from over by Mansfield way. They had bought two adjoining farms and one of the things they liked about the location was having a store where they did not have to get out onto the highway with their horse-drawn vehicles. She said, "When young Elizabeth had those twins, they came early and they weren't ready. She nearly died. Her husband came here asking for a doctor and I thought of Elsie Pierce. She's not really a doctor but what they call a Physician's Assistant but she's had midwife training. She lives only about five miles down the highway. Now when the men come to pick up stuff, they usually bring the women for a visit. Nice people."

The man looking for beer had spent 87 dollars and something on other things. Glen laughed and said he had settled for sodas. When I told Granny about it, she shook her head. "One thing Pam and I had a snarl about when she first moved up here was her wanting to sell beer. She actually bought some and brought it up here." Granny grinned. "We had quite a set-to but you need a special permit to sell alcohol of any kind and I'm not about to get one so that was that."

They did sell cigarettes, only one brand, and bags of pipe tobacco. Glen had told me where to find them in a cupboard under the counter and a sign was taped to the front of the counter. He had said, "If it wasn't for a few loyal customers, we wouldn't carry them. Granny says if the tobacco is out where people can help themselves, she has a lot of theft."

I learned that shoplifting was as much of a problem here as anywhere else. The old battle axe across the road had family who came to visit sometimes. Granny had banned the kids from coming over to play in her back yard because they refused to obey her. She had banned them from the store because they stole things. They had a policy of keeping a close eye on the adults if they came over. So I told Granny about the woman seeing Sue Ellen in the road and making a phone call alleging child neglect but not going out and doing anything. I told her about me getting mad and what I said.

Granny shook her head and said, "That's Betty Whitehall for you. It's a nice name and she can act like she's nice when she wants to. At church, she's always sweet as honey to our visiting preachers." Granny explained about their little country church not being able get a pastor so they had students who were sent from some seminary for preaching practice. The church gave them gas money and someone always asked them for Sunday dinner. Tomorrow it would be our turn.

The next morning we all went to church. If I truly had Second Sight, I would have had some notion about what was going to happen that day but I happily went off to church with no premonition.

The church was a quaint affair complete with a steeple and a bell located a mile or so down the side road. It was where the pavement ended. Two gravel roads departed in different directions from in front of the church. I had seen houses on the way to the church and several more grouped around the church indicated that Green Valley had once been a proper town. The church had a sign saying Green Valley Chapel and beside the church was a neatly mowed cemetery. The congregation contained a reasonable number of older people but younger adults were few and children were only three plus Sue Ellen and a toddler. During Sunday School, I took the toddler outside with me and Sue Ellen. Her mother looked like she could use the break. Granny taught the children's Sunday School class and today she asked a teenage girl named Gloria who normally joined the adult class to help her.

Several people asked Glen about his black eye and he really couldn't avoid telling them what happened without lying. People shook their heads but I heard someone mutter, "It figures," and I could tell they weren't saying a whole lot because they were trying to be nice.

Outside the toddler practiced climbing up and down the flight of stairs leading to the front door. At first, I stayed with him but he soon became more adept and I sat down near the bottom in a good place to catch him if he tumbled. Sue Ellen was busy with a playhouse she was arranging under a tree with rocks to mark the walls and a family of stick people who occupied it.

The preacher for today arrived and I told him they were having Sunday School inside. He introduced himself as Johnathan Underwood. He had been here before and he commented he hadn't seen me. I told him I was only temporary and he began telling me about himself. Then the toddler stumbled and I reached out to catch him. He was crying and I sat him on my lap and teased him into laughing. The young preacher-in-training kept talking to me and I saw he wanted my attention and found the child a small annoyance. He had been telling me about his various ministry opportunities and I decided I found him a small annoyance. Then I immediately felt guilty for being judgmental. Some people, especially young men, have had no experience with small children and don't know what to do with them. We need more ministers and he was a nice looking young man who could have easily chosen a different profession.

When Sunday School was over, we gathered for church. I noted Betty Whitehall setting next to the aisle in the second pew from the front. We sat on the other side of the aisle in the third pew. Glen went in first with Sue Ellen who clearly adored her daddy and I sat next to the aisle with Granny parked beside me in her wheelchair. The church had a ramp going up to a side door. Everyone wanted to meet me and Granny introduced me as Dria Davis without saying I was related but I could tell everyone assumed I was. No one asked about Pam so I concluded that she normally did not come to church.

The young preacher produced a good sermon. He was a good speaker and his topic was the need for Christians to live their religion. If it sounded a bit standardized, it was still an admirable injunction and he was young. I thought about some of the situations my father had met with in his work as a lawyer. Some cases he turned down and once he quit in the middle of a custody dispute case, returned the client's fees, and expressed the hope that she didn't even get visiting rights to her children. The woman tried to sue him.

As it was our Sunday to have the preacher for dinner, we had left a roast in a large crock pot with potatoes and carrots. Granny had supervised while I learned how to make peach cobbler.

Going home, as we approached the store, we saw flashing lights. Parked haphazardly in front of the store were three law enforcement vehicles, one State Trooper and two Carter County Sheriff cars. I saw a white sedan of some sort with Tennessee plates on it and a man and woman standing beside it.

Instantly I knew that Glen's wife, Pam, and her brother, Ray, had done something. Why did this come to me now instead this morning when it could have been prevented?

As things slowly sorted themselves out, we learned the Tennessee couple had stopped because the wife needed a restroom. When they approached the door, they saw the 'Closed for Church' sign but hearing noise inside, they had looked. They saw two people dump the large old cash register onto the floor and start pouring a bottle of something in it. They had quickly got back in their car and pulled over onto the shoulder of the main highway while calling for help. When the first siren was arriving, a jeep had come barreling out from behind the store and took off toward Green Valley. The Tennessee people had told the

State Trooper and he went looking but hadn't seen a jeep anywhere.

The Tennessee couple told the officers they had seen a man and a woman, both blonde but could give no other description. Glen looked grim and said, "Pam and her brother, Ray."

They had started their vandalism at the back and had broken all the windows out of my car and Granny's truck. They had opened two boxes in the back seat of my car but finding only clothes and books, they seemed to have lost interest. They had not bothered with the trunk for which I was exceedingly thankful.

They had broken all the windows in the back of the building and then started on the inside. They had turned over the furniture and attacked the chairs and small tables in the living room and kitchen. Everything breakable had been broken; lamps, picture frames, knick-knacks, and dishes including Granny's mother's china from the china cabinet. The china cabinet itself was smashed, probably beyond repair. So was the buffet, with it's contents scattered all over the floor and doused with stuff from the refrigerator. The bookshelf was on the floor and all the pictures had been taken off the walls and broken. They had dumped the roast, potatoes, carrots, and gravy all over the living room rug and sofa. Kitchen supplies had been poured on the books from the bookshelf and the beds in the room where Granny, Sue Ellen, and I had been sleeping. All drawers had been dumped as well as my bag and various liquids had been poured on the clothes. The mess was truly incredible.

The first thought in my mind was relief over my computer and sketch books still being locked in the trunk of my car. Computers can be replaced but I had been writing since I was ten and was lost without one. The journal I regularly kept and all of my work was on my computer. I had back-up on flash drives but they also were in the trunk of my car. My sketchbooks went back as far as my writing and were irreplaceable. I was really thankful the vandals had not taken the time to open the trunk of my car.

In the store, the cash was gone out of the register and a bottle of cooking oil had been emptied into it. They had started creating the same kind of mess in the store they had made of the living quarters.

Granny was crying over two smashed family portraits. They were her grandmother's parents and had been in matching antique oval frames. The portraits had been stomped on but had not had anything poured on them. They had suffered some damage and the antique frames were beyond repair. For some obscure reason, the destruction of the portraits made me madder than the rest of the mess.

Someone from the sheriff's office was taking photos and I retrieved my digital camera from my handbag and started taking my own pictures. We were instructed not to touch anything because they had a fingerprint person on the way.

With our dinner on the living room rug, I fed the preacher sandwiches and chips. Fortunately the vandals had not gotten to the meat case yet. When I went looking for the peach cobbler, we found it gone, dish and all. Granny said, "That sounds like Ray Williams."

One of the sheriff's deputies asked who was Ray Williams and when told, he said, "You mean you know who did all this!"

"Glen's wife left him last week," Granny explained. "She had been stealing from the business which actually belongs to me. Pam told her brother that Glen beat her, which he didn't. That's where Glen got the black eye. We are pretty sure she and her brother are our vandals."

When the officers got around to talking to the neighbors further down the road, someone said they had been outside when they heard the siren in the distance. They had seen the jeep go flying by and said it looked like one which belonged to Forrest Hunter.

Granny left with the sheriff and one of his deputies. They were going to talk to Forrest Hunter. They were gone for a while and the fingerprint woman left powder scattered all over the mess. She asked for prints from Glen, me, and even Sue Ellen and was waiting to get Granny's when she returned.

She told us Ray and Pam's prints were both already in the system. She wanted to know what Ray had touched when he was here the other day and I told her, "Nothing but the door. He came in and asked to talk to Glen outside and that was it."

She asked, "You'll swear to that?"

"Yes," I said. "I followed them to the door and saw him hit Glen. I was shocked because he hadn't sounded mad."

"Why did you follow them to the door?" she asked.

I shrugged. I wasn't wanting to mention premonitions. I said, "Ray had another man with him and I thought it was odd when he wanted to talk to Glen outside."

She nodded. "And that man was Forrest Hunter?" I could tell from her tone that she knew the man, or at least knew who he was, and for some reason her opinion was not positive.

"Yes," I said.

"Was he involved in the altercation?"

"No," I told her. "When Glen denied beating his wife, Mr. Hunter asked me if Glen had been home the night before. I said he had and I think he believed me."

"Why would he believe you?"

I hesitated and then said, "I think maybe he knows Pam well enough to know she tells lies. Granny says he's a good man and she thinks he's trying to help Ray."

She was silent while she thought it over. Whatever her conclusion was, it was expressed with an ambiguous, "Humph," and she turned away to go outside.

Granny returned carrying most of the peach cobbler. It had been photographed and released for consumption since it could not be kept in an evidence locker. "Although I was tempted to retain it," the sheriff joked. "It looks good."

Someone unearthed some styrofoam bowls and plastic spoons from the mess in the store and the cobbler was divided up and eaten on the front porch.

They had returned without Pam or Ray. Forrest Hunter had a locked gate with an intercom and a surveillance camera. He said when

Pam and Ray saw who was at the gate, they had absconded, taking a back way off his place. When he heard what had happened, he was helpful. He gave the sheriff the license and VIN number of the vehicle Pam and Ray were driving. He had taken down the numbers because he had never seen it before and Ray had a history of stealing cars. Granny had asked Forrest about the peach cobbler and he laughed, saying he should have known where it came from. They had found various items in Forrest Hunter's jeep which were not his. Among them were my car phone charger and GPS.

Granny told us Forrest Hunter had a practice of not allowing law officers onto his place without a warrant. When the sheriff had talked to him on the intercom, he had asked if they had a warrant. Granny spoke up and Forrest had let her come in and bring the sheriff with her. It had surprised the sheriff. "Apparently Hunter likes Granny," the sheriff said.

By the time everyone left, it was Sue Ellen's bedtime. She had napped briefly during the afternoon in my lap. Children need routine and familiar surroundings but the sheriff's people had been everywhere.

The rooms upstairs had not been vandalized so I gave her a bath and put her to bed in her room upstairs. The boombox downstairs was missing and not to be found anywhere in the mess. "It was among the things in Forrest's jeep," was Granny's comment. Upstairs was another one with a lullaby CD in it.

Granny had Glen carry her upstairs on his back. I saw that although Glen was average height, maybe 5 foot 10, he was stronger than he looked. I had only been upstairs to get clothes for Sue Ellen but had glimpsed a bedroom with old fashioned furniture which I thought was Granny's and one with a king-sized bed which I had assumed was used by Glen and his wife.

Three other doors had always been closed but now Granny opened one to reveal another bedroom with antique furniture for me to use. Sue Ellen's room was between it and Granny's room and had doors opening into both. The rooms had clearly been designed with small children in mind.

My bag downstairs had been dumped and my clothes were covered with what I thought was molasses and vinegar. Glen carried the boxes and bags from the back seat of my car upstairs. He didn't want anything stolen from my now open car. I had more clothes. We were all exhausted and went to bed, saying we'd tackle the mess in the morning.

I had my prayer time and then laid in bed thinking about how the problems of the Davis family here had taken my mind completely off my troubles with my step-mother. Tomorrow I was going to have to deal with my car insurance company.

My last thought as I fell asleep was wishing my Sight was either more reliable or would go away altogether. This sometimes on, sometimes off, business was a nuisance.

Chapter 4: A Secret

I didn't sleep well. I don't know if it was the unfamiliar room or the events of the day. I was inclined to think the latter as I had had no trouble at all sleeping downstairs. In the morning, we were all slow and Granny said later someone rang the bell on the store just after 7 and woke her up.

The mess was disheartening. I warned Glen and Granny that for insurance purposes, they needed to make a detailed list of all damage and take photos. Glen had a digital camera which fortunately had been upstairs.

I fed Sue Ellen cereal and took her outside. The glove box on my car was open but I found my paperwork on the floor. The sheriff's people had taken my car phone charger and GPS for evidence. I wondered when I would get them back and if I would find my other phone charger in the mess in the downstairs bedroom.

Sue Ellen played outside while I called a number which was on my insurance card. The person who answered took a report and asked me to contact my agent. I told her I was not at home. She gave me phone numbers for agents in both Van Buren and Poplar Bluff. No one was answering their phones this early.

Then Granny came to the back door and motioned me over. She said, "Can you make sure you keep Sue Ellen out here? Someone has shown up to help us clean up the mess and we don't need her underfoot. If she needs to go, take her to the old outhouse. She thinks that's fun." The outhouse was a pit toilet with three holes of assorted sizes. It was where customers who didn't meet Granny's standards for admission to her living quarters were directed.

In a little while, Glen came out with a list and some written instructions. He said, "We need some things from Poplar Bluff. Would you mind making a run? I've called the places you need to go and told them it would be you coming instead of me or Granny. Can you take Sue Ellen with you?"

I started to take Sue Ellen inside for a wash and clean clothes but when I saw people in the living room working, I hesitated. One of them was Forrest Hunter and instantly I knew Granny was trying to prevent him from seeing Sue Ellen. I didn't know how I knew this but I it felt like one of my Sight episodes. I took Sue Ellen to the outhouse and the water tap by the pump house.

Before I left, I tried calling the car insurance agent in Poplar Bluff again. He wanted me to bring the car and a copy of the sheriff's report to his office. I told him it would have to be tomorrow. It sounded to me like he didn't want to deal with it.

Granny came out to talk to me before I left. She made the effort on her walker to come outside which was confirmation of my thought about Forrest Hunter. Granny said, "We're going to be busy with this clean up for a couple of days. I was thinking you might could take Sue Ellen and go visit your relatives over at Fisk tomorrow. That would keep her from underfoot."

"The insurance agent for my car wants me to bring the car and a copy of the sheriff's report to his office. That's in Poplar Bluff. Do you think it will rain tomorrow?"

"Not suppose to. I'll see if we can get the sheriff's report today. Our insurance agent is having a fit. He didn't want anything cleaned up until he could get out here and see it sometime next week. I told him he was crazy. He's saying he isn't sure they can pay up if he doesn't personally see the mess."

Memories of growing up hearing all kinds of lawyer talk woke up. My father also handled insurance situations. I said, "Granny, give me his number. My father was a lawyer. I'll see what he tells me."

Glen came out with the number and waited while I called. I started out real nice, telling him Granny had asked me to call so we got the situation straight. It had occurred to me he might have given Granny a line because she was old but then he gave me the "I have to see the damage" edict. I said, "Mr. Crutherfield, I need to explain something. I am living here with Granny right now. My father was a lawyer so I know things. You do not have to see the damage. The sheriff's report and photographs are enough. And we have lots of witnesses. If you give too much trouble, I know how to file a law suit and I expect you know exactly how much juries hate insurance companies who won't pay up."

He started to splutter something but I cut him off. I said coolly, "Mr. Crutherfield, you can come out here right now and see the damage. Otherwise, we will make sure you get copies of the sheriff's report and the photographs," and I got off.

Glen was looking at me like I had sprouted horns. I laughed and said, "I grew up hearing lawyers tell insurance agents what's what." Then Glen laughed too.

My first stop in Poplar Bluff was McDonald's. Sue Ellen played and we ate. Then I stopped to talk to the agent for my car insurance in person and found him reasonably co-operative. I showed him the photos of my car and he said they worked with a local company. I asked if he could provide a car for me to use while they installed the glass. He asked where I was going in it and I said only out in the country near Fisk. He called and made arrangements for tomorrow. I made my rounds and filled up the SUV.

Sue Ellen fell asleep and I found a shady place under a tree to park the car and dozed off myself. When Sue Ellen woke me up, I called the store. Glen answered. They were still cleaning. I said, "Call me when you're finished for the day. I'll let Sue Ellen play until then." I had seen a park with a playground.

I called Grandmother's cousin's daughter and made arrangements to visit tomorrow.

That evening when I pulled up in front of the store to unload my cargo, Glen came out. Sue Ellen cried, "Daddy," and he unstrapped her and held her in his arms.

He looked at me and I said, "She adores you." Then I added, "She hasn't asked about her mother even once since I've been here." Then I saw tears in Glen's eyes and realized to my dismay I had hit a nerve. "I'm sorry," I said.

He said, "She's mine. Pam didn't want her and it's my name on her birth certificate. She's legally mine!"

I said, "I understand. Tomorrow I'll take her into town with me again."

He said, "I didn't know who until today. That day he came in with Ray, I was so focused on Ray, I never noticed. But he was here all day today. She was two years old before I realized anything. Somebody asked where she got her eyes. But she's mine now!"

"I've never seen her mother," I said.

"Blue eyes. Same as her brother, Ray. And the same blonde hair. I know odd things can happen but their eyes are just the same and her hair is going to be dark."

I knew he was talking about Forrest Hunter. I said, "When he was here the other day, I noticed but I thought maybe your wife was kin to him."

"No," he said. "I don't know what happened but he doesn't know about Sue Ellen."

I nodded. "I'll help keep it that way."

I was astounded to discover how much had gotten done that day. The downstairs bedroom was back to normal. I asked what had they done about the mattresses and Granny explained. "The side of this building which is closed up used to be a hotel and restaurant. It has six bedrooms with beds and furniture."

I put Sue Ellen to bed and Granny went too. She said, "It's been too long a day and I didn't sleep good last night."

My phone charger had been found and cleaned up. I put my phone to charge and Glen said, "I expect you're wondering how it happened."

I knew he was talking about Sue Ellen. I said, "You don't have to tell me anything. I know you love her and Forrest Hunter obviously has no idea she exists. Children need stability. Your wife is likely to fight you for custody and that's going to be bad enough without having some man she doesn't even know in the middle of it."

He sighed and after a long silence, he said, "I married Pam because she was pregnant and said the baby was mine." He stopped and I didn't say anything. He went on, "I dated her several times. I knew I shouldn't. She wasn't a Christian but she was beautiful and I was fascinated. One night we went to a party and they were drinking and I wanted to leave but she make me think I was acting like a prig so I stayed. Ray was there. I was drinking some kind of fruit drink which was supposed to be non-alcoholic but then I started feeling really funny and Pam laughed and said Ray had spiked my drink. I was suddenly so sleepy and she said it was because I wasn't used to alcohol. She took me into a bedroom and said to sleep it off."

Glen stopped again then he said, "I went to sleep alone with all my clothes on. I woke up in bed with Pam and we were both naked. She laughed about it and said she thought it was about time I lost my virginity. I was actually stupid enough I was with her a few more times. I was smart enough to use . . . to use protection but later she said she must have gotten pregnant the first time we were together." He paused again. "I quit seeing her but she called me and said she was pregnant and wanted me to give her money for an abortion." He shook his head. "I talked her into marrying me." He paused and then said, "I had a some money I had inherited and I got us a nice apartment in Poplar Bluff and let her spend the money. She had a lot of trouble with morning sickness and I took care of her. I thought the baby would settle her down and she had to have a cesarean so it took her a while to recover. She told me the baby was early but later, when I realized, I checked the dates and Sue Ellen weighed more than eight pounds, almost nine." Glen shook his head and said, "She knew the baby wasn't mine. I think she knew she was pregnant the first time we were together. In fact, I've even questioned in my mind if we were together that first time. And as soon as she was over the cesarean, she started running around and staying out all hours. I found a woman to keep Sue Ellen while I worked and I took care of her at home. Looking back now, I don't know why I put up with it."

He stopped and I didn't know what to say so I didn't say anything.

Then he said, "I do know why I put up with it. Sue Ellen. Babies are like miracles. They are so incredible. And I don't care who Pam was sleeping with, I'm Sue Ellen's father. I'm the one who was there when she was born. I'm the one who walked the floor with her when she had colic. I'm her father."

He was quiet and I said, "She adores you."

The next morning, even before Forrest Hunter and some neighbors arrived, the two older Amish women drove up in a buggy with young Samuel and his younger sister, Sofie.

I had a copy of the sheriff's report for my insurance agent. The sheriff had told Granny and Glen the car Ray was driving had been stolen. I took Sue Ellen and left in my windowless car even though it was really early. I told Sue Ellen we were playing a hiding game and got her to hide under a blanket. Without windows the car was cold. At one point, she pulled off the blanket and started crying. I stopped and told her she had to hide from the cold under the blanket and she didn't pull it off again. She is really a sweet child. Like all children, she sometimes gets the contraries when she's tired, but generally she is very cooperative.

I checked and found the place called Maverick Glass already open. A man named Andy said that side windows for my car were not a common order so they would not arrive until early afternoon. He also asked about the missing side mirror and when I produced it, said they could fix that too. It would be 5 pm before my car was ready.

Granny's truck insurance did not cover vandalism. I showed Andy pictures, gave him information on the make and model, and he gave me an estimate to give Granny. I put Sue Ellen and her booster seat in the loaner car which was some kind of older sedan and set off to find Grandmother's cousin.

The daughter was Maggie Stroud and she told me she had been named for my grandmother. Her mother was elderly and crippled with arthritis but when she saw me, she held out her arms for a hug and said, "Little Dria with the ringed eyes."

Then she looked at Sue Ellen and said, "And is this one yours?"

"No," I told her. "I'm just babysitting her."

Cousin Marie said, "Bring her over where I can get a good look at her," Sue Ellen looked at the woman solemnly. Cousin Marie shook her head. "It's not the same eyes but they are definitely ringed." She looked up at me and said, "She needs you to look after her."

I quickly saw Maggie was afraid I was here to take advantage of her mother in some way but as we talked, she relaxed. Cousin Marie knew my father had had money. She asked about my father's death and we talked about my step-mother trying to get my inheritance. I told her I had started here to her, looking for a place to hide. She made it clear I was welcome anytime.

I had planned on only a short visit but Cousin Marie had old family pictures and Maggie found toys for Sue Ellen. Cousin Marie had a large wall portrait of my grandmother's sister, Aunt Alice, who had the Second Sight. The portrait gave me the shivers and Cousin Marie said, "You look just like her." It was true.

She told me half a dozen stories about Aunt Alice's sightings. She said, "Alice used to pray for the Sight to be taken from her. She saw things she didn't want to see, murders and accidents and terrible things. She died in a car accident on her way to warn people about a hotel fire in which seven people died." She paused and then said, "I've always wondered why she didn't see the car accident coming but maybe God was answering her prayers in his own way."

I felt an intense sadness and then said, "I'm not sure I have the Sight. When my father was shot and killed, I didn't have any warning."

Cousin Marie said, "The Sight is like that. Alice thought it was a curse. She saw things she didn't want to see and didn't see other things which she wished she had."

The family stories said the Sight had appeared every generation going back for at least 200 years. I knew my father's sister who died at 18 months of meningitis had had the eyes.

When I was leaving, out by the car, Maggie asked me, "What about Sue Ellen? Is she really not yours?"

I smiled. My life had been so tame. I had never had anyone suspect me of having an illegitimate child before. "No," I told her, "I really am just babysitting her but her name is Sue Ellen Davis. Her family owns a store up the other side of Ellsinore called the Davis General Store. Her parents have split up and her father lives with his grandmother. The grandmother fell. She broke a rib, cracked two more, and sprained an ankle so they've hired me to help out until she's better."

Maggie observed, "She has those ringed eyes."

"I know," I replied. "I haven't been around long enough to know exactly all their family history. Her grandmother and I did discuss the family trees and decided that any relationship on the Davis side had to be quite distant."

Maggie told me where to find the cemetery where Aunt Alice was buried. On her stone was written, "I would see Jesus." In some strange way, I understood the inscription.

I picked up my car and phoned the store. Glen answered and said, "Come on home." I thought about how after just a few days, it did feel like home. Maybe it was the emotional intensity of those days.

Sue Ellen greeted her daddy with enthusiasm. He was working on the books for the store. We ate sandwiches for supper.

After Sue Ellen was in bed, Glen said to Granny, "That Forrest Hunter – I've never been around him before. You and he have talked off and on for two days about God. I've never heard you talk to anyone before like you're talking to him."

Granny said, "Forrest grew up in church and was a regular attender until his wife and son got shot. He says he had always gotten warnings about bad things happening and he thought they came from God. Then when his wife and son were shot, he didn't get a warning and he sort of lost his faith. He has suffered. I've just been trying to help him find his faith again."

"Some things you two have talked about have made me think. I feel what has happened with my marriage is the result of sin, both mine and Pam's, but Forrest doesn't see any reason for what happened to his family. I can see why he's mad at God."

"Yes, the man has suffered but suffering is our heritage. It's the consequence of Adam's sin in the Garden of Eden. And Paul wrote that suffering produces character. I think eventually Forrest will come back to God and be much stronger for his experience."

Glen said, "The man's a radical on some issues. I can see why you like him but I can also see why some people don't."

Granny smiled and said, "They don't know him. They haven't seen his heart."

I thought about the premonitions I got and how I hadn't gotten one the day Dad was killed. Did Forrest Hunter also have the Sight and was his as erratic as mine?

I went into the store to see the results of the day's work. Glen followed me and I said, "It's amazing. It's back to normal."

"Yes," he said, "the damage to the living room was the worst. Those Amish men took Granny's china cabinet and buffet home with them. They think they can repair them. They say they know an Amish man over by Rogersville who can make new picture frames for Granny just like the old ones if she gives him the pieces."

"Did your Granny raise you?" I asked.

"No, but I used to come every summer because both my parents worked. Then during my first year in college, my parents died in a car accident. My mother's parents were already dead so Gramps and

Granny were my family. When I started teaching at Poplar Bluff, I rented a place to sleep but I was up here a lot. Then I married Pam and wasn't here near as much until Gramps died and we moved up here to help Granny."

The next morning, Glen opened the store and Granny and I took Sue Ellen outside, Sue Ellen and I were working in the garden when Glen brought a woman out. I saw the strained look on his face before he said a word.

Her name was Mrs. Chandler and she was children's services. She was here because they had had a call alleging child neglect. We told her what happened and I said, "I could not believe that woman watched Sue Ellen playing alone by the highway and didn't go out and do something. I am sure there is some kind of criminal charge for that."

Mrs. Chandler said, "There is but the problem is proof. She told you but if I go ask her, she's going to deny it. When these calls come in, we guarantee anonymity. Even if the caller gives a name, we are not allowed to divulge it."

"Can you go over and give her a warning?" I asked.

Mrs. Chandler sighed. "I can try." She paused and then said, "You all look to me like you're doing a good job with the child but you really need to make sure your neighbor gets no reason to call again."

We nodded.

As I started teaching Sue Ellen how big a green bean had to be before we picked it, I thought about how thoroughly I had become a part of this family. While I was in Poplar Bluff, I should have been looking into getting a job but it hadn't even occurred to me.

Was my Second Sight telling me that this was where I belonged?

Chapter 5: Another Secret

The next morning after breakfast, Granny and Glen wanted to talk about something. I thought maybe they were finding ten dollars a day too much but that wasn't it at all. Granny said, "With all those people here to help clean up the mess, they were asking about the part of this building which we aren't using. Running a restaurant like we used to do is too much. We would need all new kitchen equipment and too much help. But someone suggested a bed and breakfast. We can hire part time help if we need it. What do you think?"

I went on a tour of the closed off part of the building. The huge front area used to be the restaurant. Turning it into a shop selling quilts, handcrafts, and antiques had been suggested. Under the open stairway at the back of the restaurant area were a pair of restrooms with attractive brass plaques reading "Ladies" and "Gentlemen."

The old restaurant and the store both had extremely high ceilings while the parts at the back of the building had been made into two floors, both with what I estimated to be 9 or 10 foot ceilings. Behind the store was the living quarters. Behind the restaurant downstairs were a lounge, a kitchen, and a storage room and upstairs were the old hotel bedrooms.

The kitchen was interesting. The appliances were all old enough to qualify as antiques but Granny said she thought they all still worked. They had legs and Lady chased something underneath a huge cook stove and it squeaked when she caught it. Granny said, "We always kept the floor clear. It made pest control a lot easier."

I said, "Maybe you could just do breakfast in your own kitchen. I think you'd need to add a dishwasher but how many people could you possibly have at once?" Behind the kitchen was a storage room with shelves, now empty.

Upstairs were six bedrooms. They had twin beds with antique iron frames, dressers. small tables, and comfortable looking chairs. Some of the chairs were a bit shabby. Three of the bedrooms had double windows looking out over the roof of the back porch. The other three rooms also each had double windows but they looked out into the restaurant area. The stairs were underneath them and Granny said they could be used for escape in case of fire.

In the past, the bedrooms upstairs in the living quarters side were sometimes also rented out. Between the two hallways was a door which could be unlocked.

Glen said they had asked the Amish men about repairing the outside stairway at the back on the empty side of the building. "Grandpa kept the other one in good repair but this one needs a little work."

It would take a lot of work and some money but Granny thought the unused space could be reopened. Back downstairs, we discussed it. Granny said, "I have some money. Herb and I never lived high on the hog. We never thought the government would take care of us when we got old. I could put some money into this project and it should make money and some of the women around here would be happy for part time work. We'd need to advertise but Forrest said we can do that on the internet now. That and a good new sign would draw in trade and six rooms aren't really much." Granny paused and looked at me. "We need to do some cost assessment but if we go ahead with it, would you be willing to stay and help run it?" she asked.

I knew instantly I wanted to do it. But it was a commitment. I said, "Let me think about it. I'm really interested but I should pray about it."

Glen took Granny's truck and went into town to get the windows fixed. He took the coolers to restock and he took Sue Ellen with him. Granny and I were running the store. I was getting pretty adept at making sandwiches by the time Forrest Hunter came in after one.

He started talking to Granny and I decided it was his real reason for being here. The discussion topic was "Why does a good God let bad things happen?" As it was something I have wrestled with myself, I was interested. Forrest believed in a creator God but doubted His concern with individual people.

Granny's position was that, as children of Adam, we were all heirs to suffering but God did care about us individually and only let bad things happen for reasons which we did not understand. Granny was sensitive to Forrest's grief over his wife and son. She said, "Maybe God saw something in the future which made it better for Him to take them home to heaven. I do believe they are with Him now and not suffering." I could see Forest was interested in what Granny had to say.

Later I found myself bringing up Job, the righteous man God allowed Satan to test. After my father died, I had found Job's story comforting.

Granny quoted Paul from the first chapter of Second Corinthians where he said we suffer so we might comfort others who suffer and through it we learn to depend on God and not on ourselves.

Forrest thought the whole idea of "God will take care of me" was a cop-out. He said too many people were refusing to take responsibility for their own lives and wanting others, including the government, to take care of them.

Forrest was radical about the government. He said the government was trying to control our lives. He said our original constitution had been intended to strictly limit the powers of the government. He said a major problem was too many people were asking the government to take care of them because they did not want to take responsibility for themselves, and in doing that, they were giving the government too much power.

He thought everyone should carry a gun and be allowed to use it.

Granny asked what about people like Ray? "Do you think Ray should be allowed to carry a gun?"

Forrest sighed and then said, "If other people were legally allowed to deal with Ray as needed, he would not be the problem he has become. He would have either changed his ways or be dead."

I thought about my father's killer running around loose on bail. I did see Forrest's point.

Forrest hung a flyer and left some in a stack. He was running another survival training course soon.

After he was gone, it felt like an empty daycare center after all the children left, deflated and a little forlorn. I thought about it. Forrest was interesting and intense. Something about him generated electricity. He was an attractive man.

That thought jolted me as much as his eyes had done the first time I saw him. A picture leaped into my mind of me in a soft, flowing old-fashioned wedding dress and him standing facing me, looking into my eyes with love.

"*No!*" I told myself. "*No silly nonsense like that. He's too much older and he's not marriage material. He's still grieving over losing his first wife. He doesn't want another wife or he would have married Pam. Don't even think about him!*"

As a change of subject, I said to Granny, "I'm glad Glen took Sue Ellen with him."

Granny said, "Glen told me you knew." She sighed. "I didn't know he knew she wasn't his and I sure wasn't going to tell him. He had never said anything about it and he had no idea who the man was until the day before yesterday when Forrest came to help us clean up." She shook her head. "I'd like to deal with that woman." Her voice was grim.

I thought about it. "I'd help you," I said.

"We can try our best but I don't know what Forrest would do if he saw Sue Ellen. He's such a vigorous man. He's inclined to take action and tell the law to go soak its head. What he wouldn't know is how much Glen loves that child."

"Glen told me he didn't care who Pam had been sleeping with, it was his name on her birth certificate and he was the one who had taken care of her. I'll do my best to help you keep Forrest from seeing her," I promised.

Later it occurred to me that both Granny and I were assuming Forrest would want Sue Ellen. Granny knew him but I didn't, yet somehow I knew she was right.

We started discussing the bed and breakfast thing again. "Forrest had a suggestion. Instead of just a store in the old dining room, we could divide up the space and rent it to people for individual stalls. I've seen those kind of places but I don't really know how they work. Glen's having a look at one in Poplar Bluff today."

With Granny's directions, I cooked supper and Glen came home. He unloaded supplies for the store while I took charge of Sue Ellen. She had a new stuffed toy, a dog almost as big as she was. At 7 o'clock, we closed the store and ate supper. Glen told us about his visit to Somewhere in Time in Poplar Bluff. He said the man who was running it had been willing to give information. He found out booths usually are something like 8 to 10 feet by 8 or 10 feet but in older buildings, the booths are often irregular sizes and in that case, the owner might rent booths according to size. Then Glen talked about the usual rents in the Poplar Bluff area. He said, "I can see it would be a real money maker for the owner. Up here we might not can charge as much but it still should make a good profit. I was told the real trick is to attract the right vendors for your booths. I think we need to check out each place in the area and talk to people."

That night, I prayed earnestly. I knew that because of my relationship with my own grandmother, I had easily attached to Granny. It was possible my own uncertain situation was causing me to latch on to what looked like security. It was very possible I was seeing what I wanted to see instead of what was really there. I needed more than my own limited perceptions and yearnings. I prayed earnestly.

The next morning, a man appeared from Granny's insurance company. He was not her agent but someone else whose job was to go around assessing damages and deciding how much compensation should be paid. We explained to him about the neighbors coming in and helping clean up the mess but we had photos and detailed notes. I said to the man, "We would have lost business if we had waited to clean up. This business depends on customers who come here because of location and accessibility. People know the only time they really can't get anything here is Sunday morning during church time. That's why the vandals came then."

We had replaced the destroyed kitchen table and chairs with some from the old restaurant and Mr. Rogers ("Call me Jim") settled there with our lists and photographs. Glen asked me to stay with Granny while he dealt with the store. He said I knew more about dealing with insurance companies than he did.

Jim Rogers eventually said, "I'm impressed with your documentation. I really would not have believed how much damage was done if you had not taken such detailed photos." He was sorting out the damage into living quarters and business. He started asking questions and making notes.

He told Granny her building was woefully under-insured so it was fortunate the vandals had not set it on fire. Her policy had a thousand dollar deductible so expenses for replacing the broken windows would only be covered for the amount over that. During clean up, they had taped plastic sheeting over the openings for rain protection.

The contents of the store were ensured for twenty-five thousand dollars so the losses there were covered except for the deductible. When he saw the photo of the cash register, Granny told him they did not know yet if it was ruined or not. John Miller had taken it home with him to clean. Since its insides were mechanical, not electrical, he thought it would be fine once it was cleaned. I saw the man write "cash register repair - $200" on his list and knew Granny probably thought the machine was not worth that much but I thought I would check on-line later. It was a lovely antique and I did hope it would survive its misadventure.

Granny's living quarters only had five thousand dollars insurance on contents. Jim Rogers said, "I need a list for my records but frankly, there is easily more than six thousand dollars in damages here."

When he was finished, I asked him to give suggestions as to how much insurance Granny actually needed so we toured the whole place. I told him we were considering opening it back up and running a bed and breakfast and selling handcrafts and antiques. He stood in the middle of the old restaurant and said, "It's a great idea. This ceiling with its old metal tiles is fantastic. Have you thought about the fact that this ceiling is high enough you could build a mezzanine and create more selling space? "

"No," I told him. "We are only just now starting to consider the whole idea."

He said, "Those rooms having windows looking out into this area are interesting. It's the sort of whimsical touch tourists like."

I told him Granny said it had been done to provide possible escape in case of fire.

"Practical," he responded. "Let's have a look at the cellar." I had not known about the cellar but behind a locked door in the storage room off the old kitchen were some stairs. To my surprise, the cellar was dry and in good shape. Jim Rogers walked all around inspecting the foundations, the thick stone wall down the middle, and the massive stone pillars which supported the floors overhead. He said, "They don't build stuff like this anymore. This one was well done and is in good shape."

We also inspected the attic reached by stairs behind a door in the upper hall I had assumed was another closet. We noted a couple of places where the roof needed attention. Jim Rogers said, "This roof is tin. You may have trouble finding someone to do it."

I said, "Those Amish will know how."

He told Granny she should get new wiring installed in the part of the building which was now closed but the building alone was worth two hundred and fifty thousand dollars. He said, "I'd advise you to carry at least two hundred thousand dollars insurance on it. Get that roof fixed. When you open for business, call your agent. You will need more liability insurance."

As he was leaving, outside he told me, "If I tell you something, will you never say I said it?" I was puzzled. The insurance agent Granny had called was in Ellsinore but his company had another one in Van Buren. I understood. He was directing us to someone more competent, which action would get him into trouble if known.

While we dealt with Mr. Rogers, I had given Sue Ellen some play dough I had made for her. She talked to herself quietly while she created people, houses, pets, a garden – in short, her world. When the insurance man left, Sue Ellen was still playing with her play dough. Suddenly she threw something across the room and said, "Go away! And don't come back!"

Was she mad at the insurance agent? "Sue Ellen?" I asked softly, wanting to calm her down, "Who should go away and not come back?"

"Mommy!" she said.

"Why are you mad at Mommy?" I asked.

"Thee'th mean to Daddy. Thee thaid thee hate'th Daddy. Thee hit-ed Daddy and thee thaid thee hated him."

I said, "Well, that wasn't a nice thing to say, was it?"

"Thee thaid bad wowds and thee hit-ed Daddy and made blood."

Did I understand right? "She hit your daddy and he was bleeding?"

"Yeth. Thee hit Daddy when he told her to thtop taking pictuweth."

It was a difficult word for her and I asked, "Your mommy was taking pictures and your daddy told her to stop and then she hit him?"

"Yeth. He took her camawa."

"Your daddy took your mother's camera away from her? What was she taking pictures of?"

"Thee wath taking pictuweth of me naked. Daddy made her thop. He thayth nobody ith supposed to take pictuweth of me naked. And he thayth my pee-pee plathe is pwivate and nobody ith thuppothed to take pictuweth of it. He thayth nobody ith thuppothed to touth it."

I stood still in complete shock. Then I said, "I don't think your mother is coming back."

I hesitated, thinking. When I was bathing Sue Ellen, I had been teaching her to bath herself and I always had her wash her own "pee-pee place." I wasn't sure if I should do the asking but we had to know. "Sue Ellen, has anybody been touching your pee-pee place?"

She looked at me and said, "He thiad it wath a thecwet and I wath not thuppothed to tell Daddy."

"Who said it was a secret?" I asked with chills running down my spine.

"Uncle Way," she said.

"Sue Ellen," I said, "did he tell you not to tell me the secret?"

"No," she said.

"Did Uncle Ray touch you on your pee-pee place?"

"Yeth," she said, "and I told him he wath not thuppothed to touth me thewe."

I had to know how far it went. I asked, "Sue Ellen, did Uncle Ray hurt you at all?"

"No," she said. "He like to tickle me."

"When Uncle Ray touched your pee-pee place, did you have any clothes on?"

She said, "I had my panieth on."

"Did he put his hand in your panties?"

"He was tickling me and he twied to take my panieth off and tickle my pee-pee place. I told him to thtop."

"Did he stop?" I asked.

"Yeth," she said. "Mommy thaid I'd tell Daddy and then Uncle Way thaid it was a thecwet and I wath not thuppothed to tell Daddy."

"So your mother was there when this happened?" I asked.

"Yeth," she said.

I said, "Sue Ellen, your Daddy was exactly right. Nobody is supposed to touch your pee-pee place."

I paused, wondering how much she could take in at one time but the issue needed to be talked about. I could remind her again later. "Sue Ellen, nobody is supposed to tell you something is a secret and not to tell your Daddy. If anyone ever tells you that again, you keep quiet then – but as soon as you see your Daddy, you tell him about it. Okay?"

She was playing with her play dough again so I didn't know if she was listening but she said, "Okay."

That afternoon, while Sue Ellen was napping, I told Granny and Glen. Glen said, "I'll kill him!"

I said, "Glen, if you do that, they'll arrest you and who will get Sue Ellen?"

He looked pained and torn and distraught.

I said, "You telling her no one was supposed to touch her there was excellent. She told him to stop. I've told her if anyone ever tells her not to tell you something, then she should tell you as soon as she sees you. It may make keeping Christmas presents a secret difficult but that's far better than having her not tell you something she should."

Glen said incident with the camera had happened just before they moved up here. Ray had stayed with them a few days. Glen was so upset, he had tears in his eyes. "I can't believe how little Pam cares about Sue Ellen!"

Granny said, "People think all this sexual abuse of children is new but it's just that now the news people talk about it. It happened when I was young too. We had one family living near us that everyone knew to keep their children away from. And my mother told me what was what, not as young as Sue Ellen, but before I started school. I think people used to talk to their children more than they do now with everyone watching TV and on their phones and computers all the time."

Glen said, "Pam is not coming back! I don't care what she says, I'm not having her around Sue Ellen. I know I should file for a divorce but if I do, she'll probably fight for custody unless I pay her off and I don't have anything left to pay her off with."

The rest of the day was quiet. I knew Glen was brooding. I took Sue Ellen out to the garden and she had a lot of fun even if I had a hard time keeping my mind on it. I cooked supper. She built a playhouse out of her Mega Blocks for her dolls. I noticed her dolls were all the old-fashioned type, no beauty queens, and she had a boy rag doll that was always "Daddy."

That night when she was in bed, I wrote a poem. I started writing when I was 10 and Mama died. I wrote short stories and poetry. My stories are all fantasy. In them a little girl named Mary Ellen has a fairy friend who helps her catch thieves, find kidnappers, and right the wrongs of the world. My fairy world had always been my retreat. My poems were where I expressed my emotions. Sue Ellen's revelation had provoked a lot of emotion.

Sunday came around and Forrest appeared when it was time for us to leave for church. His arrival was so unexpected, he almost saw Sue Ellen but it was Granny he wanted. He had come to guard the place while we went to church. Granny told him, "How thoughtful of you."

Down the road, she said, "Forrest really is a good man."

Glen didn't say anything and I didn't either.

The preacher this week was another young man who also wanted my attention. This one was very tall and thin with a weak chin and mousy hair. He peered at the world through thick glasses and his speaking style was bland, although his subject matter was good and his sermon well organized and interesting with good illustrations. On the way home, Granny said, "I wonder if he could get contact lenses? And he needs to put some fire in his sermons." It was so exactly on target, I found myself chuckling.

I was not surprised by the attention of the young preachers. I knew I was considered pretty. Along with my ringed eyes, I had thick dark hair which curled just enough, pleasant face features, and I had developed nicely with no weight problems. I knew physical beauty has no moral virtue. It was just the luck of drawing the right genes. My friend, Regina, didn't eat any more than I did but somehow her body made fat and mine didn't. In one of her letters from Calcutta, she wrote, "My body was designed to live on rice and lentil soup. I've lost weight and I'm healthier than I've ever been."

At Green Valley Chapel, I had no competition except the teenager, Gloria, who was shy and gawky. I decided to get to know the girl better. She probably needed a Christian friend.

At home, I helped Granny out of the SUV and Glen drove off with Sue Ellen. They were going to McDonald's in Van Buren. We found Forrest at the kitchen table typing into a laptop computer. "I got your password off your router," he said. "I hope you don't mind."

"I don't mind," Granny said and with Sue Ellen safely out of the way, she asked Forrest to stay for dinner. With Glen and Sue Ellen gone, we had plenty of food.

Forrest asked if anything had turned up missing which they had not found in his jeep besides the cash.

Forrest then expressed the thought that Glen would be divorcing Pam. Granny said exactly what Glen had told me, that Pam would fight him for Sue Ellen hoping he would pay her off. Granny said, "Glen had about two hundred fifty thousand dollars he had inherited from his folks when he married her. By the time they moved up here, she had gone through it all, run up debts Glen is still paying off, and was griping all the time about money. I knew she was stealing right away but she was trying not to get caught so it wasn't very much until she started letting her friends in on it. The worst was letting them get gas and not pay. We don't really make anything on gas anyway. We just sell it as a convenience for our customers who don't go into town. It's delivered by the same people who deliver to a few farms around here which have their own tanks."

During dinner, Forrest and Granny discussed divorce. Granny, of course, was not in favor of it generally but thought it was sometimes necessary. Glen's situation was one of those.

Forrest was arguing for a much more liberal standard in which divorce was justified if the couple were not happy together.

Granny alleged some people were never happy regardless and making divorce too easy would lead to people not even trying to work out their differences.

As I listened, I found myself enjoying the debate. And I was aware again of what an attractive man Forrest was. I thought, "*He's probably got women lined up waiting to climb in bed with him.*" My thoughts did not usually run in the gutter and I scolded myself strongly.

Then Forrest suddenly said to me, "Dria, what do you think? You've been listening but you haven't said a word."

"I think you like a lively discussion and you say things just to get Granny going." I don't know where it came from but as soon as I said it, I knew it was true.

Forrest laughed. "I should know better than to try to ask an awkward question of someone with your eyes."

"What have my eyes got to do with it?" I asked.

"You see beyond the surface. You see through things." I looked into his eyes and saw he was no longer laughing. He was both direct and completely serious.

Later when Granny excused herself for a few minutes, he asked me, "Where did you get those eyes?"

"They run in my family," I said. "The family legends say they are accompanied by the Second Sight."

"Do you have it?" he asked. "Do you have Second Sight?"

"I'm not sure," I said. "Sometimes I get premonitions. Sometimes I know things which logically I shouldn't know. But also sometimes I don't see things which are obvious and sometimes something really bad is going to happen and I don't see it coming."

He nodded.

I had to ask. "Is it like that for you too?"

He sighed. "Sometimes I hate it. I know things I don't want to know and then I don't know things I really need to know."

I nodded. "That about sums it up."

"Tell me about it running in your family," he said and I told him about Aunt Alice. Then I told him our family stories said it went back more than two hundred years into Scotland.

He said, "No one told me anything until I was 18 and went into the military. The men in my unit called me Cat Eyes. They said I had the instincts of a wildcat and over there in the middle-east, it seemed like I could smell trouble."

"You didn't stay in the military," I said.

He shook his head. "Our government is an idiot and our military is mostly run by idiots," he said. "I expect you've heard that joke about committees being the only known form of life with twelve stomachs and no brain. Our government is like a committee, lots of talk and it eats well, but it's real short on brains."

I had to smile. It so exactly explained some things the government did.

"Do the eyes run in your family?" I asked.

"My grandmother has them," he said, "but we don't know anything back beyond her. She was a newborn baby when she was found one Sunday morning in a church over near Van Buren. It was during the Depression. Someone said they had seen some people traveling through but no one ever really found out anything."

Granny returned and we talked about other things.

As Forrest was leaving, I went to the door with him to lock it behind him. He said to me, "Dria, you have an interesting mind. Would you go out with me this evening?"

My heart leaped. I found him so attractive but I knew with no doubt whatsoever, I should not get involved with him. I smiled at him and said, "I've been given compliments before but no one ever admired my mind. However, I need to stay here. Granny still needs me and I was hired to take care of her and Sue Ellen."

"When is your day off?" he asked.

He was so direct. "I'm not sure," I answered. "We are still sorting some things out."

"Granny has my number," he said and left.

Granny said, "I heard him ask you out. Do you not like him?"

I said, "I shouldn't get involved with him. He's Sue Ellen's biological father and we really don't want him hanging around."

"But you like him," Granny said.

"He's an attractive man but he's older than me and . . . ." I really did not know what to say.

Granny said, "I understand. He's like fire. It gives light and warmth but it can burn too."

"Exactly," I agreed.

Chapter 6: Kidnapping

On Sunday evening, Granny and Glen decided they would do a complete feasibility study on turning the old restaurant into an antique store divided into booths which would be rented to individuals. In the meantime, Granny said we could probably do a bed and breakfast this summer without doing anything else. We could let the guests use our upstairs bathroom which was right next to the door into the hallway where the old hotel rooms were located. Granny said, "We only have six rooms and we don't have to rent them all at once."

Granny called Gloria's mother and asked if they would like some paid cleaning work. They had helped with the vandalism clean-up. So Monday morning we started on the old hotel bedrooms upstairs.

Granny came up the stairs on her bottom. She was getting around much better and said she was about ready to throw the walker away. It amazed me how well preserved things were. Granny said, "I tried. Moth balls and cedar shavings go a long way and our closets are all cedar lined. Rugs had been rolled up and stored in the closets. Out in the hall was a large linen closet, cedar lined and full of linens including curtains.

Granny had unlocked the door in the upstairs hall which connected to the hall in the old hotel. We were using water from our bathroom but Granny talked to someone who promised to come tomorrow and see what needed to be done to use the hotel's bathrooms. It had two upstairs, both equipped with old-fashioned footed bathtubs. Granny told us in the hotel days, one of them had been reserved for ladies only. The bathrooms were so big I suggested Granny ask the man if it was possible to install a shower in one of them. Downstairs were restrooms and we always had the outhouse out back.

Window washing looked like it was going to be a matter of climbing out onto the porch roof until Granny showed us how they worked. The bottom sashes had ropes in the sides with weights to make them easy to slide up and down. They had large screws for taking them apart to repair the ropes and clean the glass. It was ingenious and while we worked, Granny made a list of needed repairs.

After lunch, an electrician arrived. He was a man the insurance adjuster dad recommended. He prowled all over the building, going down to the cellars and up to the attics. He had ideas and made some suggestions. He said the old wiring had been well done back in the 40's but he was astounded it still worked and it needed to be completely replaced. He gave Granny an estimate but wrote right on it that if they encountered any major problems hidden from his view, it could cost more. He said, "I've allowed for some of that and I could see enough so I really don't expect anything big to turn up but I've had it happen. I found a colony of honey bees once. We had to take an entire wall down to get them out." We had told him about the antique store idea and he included an extra section for doing electrical outlets for each booth. He said it was far better for him to do it all at one time. He said he could allow for a mezzanine later.

As we worked, with Sue Ellen 'helping,' I had gotten to know Gloria better. She had just turned 16 and was between her sophomore and junior years in high school. I remembered well how awkward I had felt at that age. She wore glasses and was very tall and skinny. I saw her awkwardness was partly caused by her attempts to look smaller by hunching over. When she relaxed, she was much more graceful.

I told her, "I really envy your height. You should strut like a queen. Models are all tall and skinny like you."

She said, "I'm taller than all the boys in my class."

I said, "Who cares about the boys in your class? They're too young. Girls grow up faster than boys. At 16, you want to take a look at guys two or three years older than you."

"But that means they're seniors or even out of school."

"Of course," I said. "But don't you find boys your age immature?"

She giggled and said, "Yes, really they are so silly."

Later I asked her mother if it was possible for Gloria to get contacts instead of glasses. Her mother said, "Her eye doctor suggested it but she didn't want them. I don't know why."

"She's hiding," I said. "She feels awkward being so tall but models are all tall and skinny, just like Gloria. She could be striking if she would walk tall. She's actually an attractive girl."

By the end of the day, we had a lot done and during the evening, conversation was all about what else we needed to do. Glen planned to move his king-sized bed into the room from which we had taken the mattresses for our downstairs bedroom. Granny said in the linen closet were arm covers and head pieces for the wing-back chairs as well as curtains and bed linens for all the rooms.

I had not told Granny I would stay but I did know I wanted to very much. However, I wanted some kind of clear confirmation from God about it. I told Granny I would stay for the summer and we would see after that. She nodded and said, "By the end of this summer, we'll know if we want to go on with the bed and breakfast. We can run it through the winter if there's customers. Those rooms are heated in the winter."

I thought about the huge boiler I had seen in the cellar. The building still had radiators in each room and a whole array of them in the store and old restaurant. Granny had told me they still worked and were turned on each winter. She said, "We've been heating the old hotel and restaurant area each winter. Herb knew how it worked and he said turning it off would make the building deteriorate so we left it on each winter."

We worked all week on the bed and breakfast project with Sue Ellen in the middle of it. I started teaching her children's songs which she absorbed with glee.

The plumber looked at everything and said he was surprised at how good it all looked. The water to the hotel bathrooms and kitchen had been shut off but Granny said her husband had always turned it on each spring and checked it for leaks. The plumber inspected the septic tank and the water pump and said, "Probably adequate."

The old water heater for the hotel and restaurant had run on propane gas and he suggested replacing it with small electric things mounted on the wall which kicked on and produced hot water when needed. He said they would be more economical. He and our electrician would consult.

Wednesday Glen went into town for supplies and the next morning, the Amish came after their stuff. They thought the antique store was a good idea and said if we did it, they would rent a booth, maybe even two. When we told them about the suggested mezzanine, they looked it over and started measuring and sketching.

The men were ready to start work on the north stairs. So we had people busy everywhere when Forrest Hunter appeared again. I saw his jeep at the side of the building and immediately made plans for keeping Sue Ellen out of sight. He wanted to see the place and in avoiding him, I ghosted up and down stairs and finally up to the attic. I told Sue Ellen it was a hiding game and she giggled. She had never been to the attic before. It wasn't dark because of the dormer windows in the roof and the double windows on the ends, just like the hotel bedrooms. Granny said in the lumber camp days, it had been used as a dormitory for lumberjacks.

On Thursday, Granny and I were upstairs sorting out linens for the hotel rooms when Glen called up the stairs for me. A man and a woman had seen my old Ford Tempo out back and were interested to buy it. I said, "I'm sorry but I'm not interested in selling it."

As soon as I saw the couple, I had a mental image of handcuffs come in my mind. I had never had that happen before. They were both stocky and looked physically fit. They had a few tattoos and he had a shaved head and an earring but they didn't look nearly as wild as the girl with the purple spiked hair who had stolen her grandmother's car.

They were wearing matching tan shirts and trousers which reminded me of law enforcement uniforms. They wanted to look at my car. I said, "I'm sorry but my father bought it new and took good care of it. I'm not interested in selling it."

They tried to talk old cars and said they wanted to look at it just for interest. I said, "I'm sorry. I'm supposed to be working and I was in the middle of something. If you want an old Ford Tempo, look on the internet."

I went back upstairs but kept looking out the back windows to make sure they were not where they didn't belong. Later I asked Glen about them. He said, "They pulled in and parked at the side of the building. They were driving a jeep with California plates, like yours, and my first thought was they were tourists. We get a fair number of them in the summer. Then I heard Spot start barking out back. She's not normally much of a barker so I looked and they were in the drive by the porch and she was objecting to their presence. I told them to come around front, the dog was there to keep people out."

I said, "Something about them made me uncomfortable. They were a little pushy but I think it was more than that. Why would they be so interested in my car? It's too old for usual buyers but not old enough for antique car people."

During the night after we were all asleep, I was awakened by Spot barking. She and the cats slept in a pile in the old stables. She had never barked before in the middle of the night. Granny had also woke up so I went to look. Spot had gone out by the highway, still barking, and I heard a vehicle door slam and then an engine start up over where she was barking. I tried to get a look at the vehicle but I was too late. For some reason, that couple who had wanted to buy my car came to mind. Spot greeted me happily and I petted her and told her what a good dog she was.

Granny said, "We used to keep a gun down in the store but when Glen moved up here with Sue Ellen, I put it away in the closet of my bedroom upstairs. I didn't want the child to get a hold of it. Maybe we need to find a good place to keep it down here."

So the next day, Glen put the shotgun on the highest shelf behind the cash register. He said, "It isn't very handy but Sue Ellen cannot reach it and it's out of sight."

The next Sunday, Forrest was coming again to guard the store while we went to church. I suggested taking Sue Ellen and going to visit my grandmother's cousin. I called her and left in my car with Sue Ellen before Forrest arrived.

We went to church with Cousin Marie and her daughter, Maggie. The church had a children's program and Sue Ellen happily joined the other children. The preacher was a short, tubby man who was an unexpectedly good speaker. At the end of the service, I met his wife who was equally short and round with her face beaming good will and contentment.

Sue Ellen and I had been invited for Sunday dinner and we enjoyed fried chicken with the normal side dishes. When Maggie produced a peach cobbler, I told them about our vandals and my peach cobbler's journey to Forrest Hunter's and then home again.

Cousin Marie was concerned. Was where I was worked not safe? I told her there had never been any danger of me being attacked. Our vandals had come at a time when they knew we would all be at church. I told her we now had a shotgun handy in the store if we needed it and someone had volunteered to guard the store on Sunday mornings when we were all gone. Cousin Marie said, "If it ever gets to where you aren't safe up there, you can come down here."

I told her I appreciated the offer and began telling them about the bed and breakfast and maybe antique store. I told them I had been asked to stay on and help run it. They told me where to find some antique malls-flea markets just outside Poplar Bluff. They were open on Sunday afternoons so I decided to go have a look.

They told me where to find five and suggested which one to see first so I set off planning to spend a couple of hours looking them over. My first stop was called Country Bumpkins. The booths were 10 feet by 10 feet and the owner had decorated the walls and rafters above the booths with all sorts of interesting old items. In a booth on the last isle, I found a big box of the larger sized Lego Blocks that Sue Ellen was now old enough to use.

When I checked out, I noticed the two ladies running the place were using a computer, typing in the information from the tag on the Legos. I started asking questions. They told me they entered the booth number, item number, price, and a short description of every item sold. The computer not only added taxes but would print a receipt if I wanted one. I did. I wanted to see what it looked like. They said the computer also printed up lists at the end of the week of what each vendor sold and how much money the store owed them. They told me if I came in tomorrow, the store owner would be there and he could tell me more.

When we arrived, a lot of cars were in the parking lot and we had parked down a sidewalk at the end of the building away from the door. At the car, I was fastening Sue Ellen into her seat belt when I realized two people were coming at me from opposite sides between my car and the pick-up truck parked next to me. It was the couple who had wanted to look at my car and I knew immediately something was badly wrong.

The woman was holding an object in her hand and she said, "Do what we say or I'll tase you."

The daycare where I worked had held a training class for us staff once on dealing with kidnappers, terrorists, and crazies. I didn't wait to see what they were going to say. I slammed the car door to protect Sue Ellen and started screaming for help. The woman tased me and I collapsed in the man's arms. They got on either side of me and put me in their jeep and handcuffed me. They rolled me onto the floor and chained me to a car seat. They threw a blanket over me. I was wondering how long before I would be able to scream again when they started the jeep and left the parking lot.

They stopped and let a car pass before pulling out onto another road. When they turned right again in less than a minute, I knew we were on Highway 60 going west. I felt a curve and knew we were taking the business route into town.

Since they hadn't gagged me, I knew they didn't plan to take me anywhere where people could hear me. I started praying for someone to find Sue Ellen right away.

I heard other traffic. When we stopped at a traffic light, I yelled, "Are two crazy? You've left a three-year-old alone in a car in the summer sun. She could die!" I figured we were in Poplar Bluff but when we stopped and they turned off the engine of the jeep, I couldn't hear anyone. The woman got out and I took the blanket off my face. I was chained to the seat so I could not even sit up but I said to the man, "Why are you doing this?"

He said, "Young people with drug problems shouldn't run away from their family who's trying to help them."

My fear of being held as a sex slave disappeared and I said, "If you two were hired by Belle Davis, you're in trouble. I don't have a drug problem. She's trying to get my inheritance."

"She told us you'd say that. There isn't any inheritance. Her lawyer was with her and he said so."

"That lawyer is sleeping with her and hopes to share the money."

"You tell a good story," he said and the woman came back with two duffle bags which she put in the back of the jeep.

She unchained me but left my cuffs on. She pulled me roughly out of the jeep and I saw we were outside a row of motel rooms. The motel building was built on a slope and I realized the rooms on the second story were facing the other way and the front of the motel would open there at ground level. Here at the back, no one was around.

I saw the woman had added patches to her clothing which made it look like the uniform of a sheriff's deputy. When she turned, I could read "Deputy Sheriff - Kern County California." Then I saw the man was adding them to his clothing.

The woman said to me, "You are going to ride in the back seat in cuffs. We are law enforcement officers returning you to California. It will do you no good what-so-ever to tell anyone anything else. If you're smart, you'll keep quiet and do what your told. If you're good, we'll feed you. If you aren't, you'll go hungry."

I knew they had it covered. I asked if they would make a phone call to be sure someone got Sue Ellen out of my car. I said, "She's only 3 and she missed her nap. She'll go to sleep and she could easily die from the heat."

The woman punched 911 and said, "There's a small child left in a car in the parking lot of a Flea Market called Country Bumpkins." They must have asked her where the flea market was located because she said, "Off of T Highway near the Highway 60 junction." After another pause, she said, "That's good. No, I didn't see who left her there." She hung up.

"Thank you," I said. I guessed someone had already noticed Sue Ellen.

I asked to use the restroom. It was a typical inexpensive motel room with out-of-date décor but looked clean.

They put me in the middle of the back seat of the jeep, away from door handles and windows. I was in handcuffs with a chain which limited my movements so I could not lift my hands higher than my waist. No grabbing my captors from behind. My feet were in leg-irons and anchored so I could not kick out windows or anything useful like that. I decided they were pros.

As we drove away from the motel, they took some route which did not take us through the busiest part of Poplar Bluff. We were soon on 67 Highway going north. I could not think of any way anyone would figure out what happened to me. My purse with my cell phone was in my car. I had put it inside along with the box of Legos so my hands were free to fasten Sue Ellen into her seat belt.

I started praying.

Chapter 7: Stopping at Four Corners

North of Poplar Bluff, we took the ramp for Highway 60 West. We would be going right by the Davis General Store. From where I was sitting, I could see the man was driving a steady 65 miles per hour. We were not going to get pulled over for speeding. A few vehicles passed us and we passed one. I tried to search each one for a familiar face but it was not easy to see the drivers. Eventually a car passed with a child on the passenger side looking out the window. The car had one of those zombie drivers who sets their vehicle on cruise control and never speeds up or slows down so it was passing us at a speed Granny called 'molasses in January.' I had plenty of time to stick my tongue out at the boy and make all kinds of faces. He gave no sign of seeing me. The jeep had well-tinted side windows and I had already suspected no one could see inside.

 As we were approaching the Davis General Store, I thought, it's too bad I can't just ask them to drop me off there. Then it occurred to me a little humor might help, so as we approached the intersection, I said, "Just let me out at the next corner."

 The woman's head jerked around and she said, "You're a real smart-ass, aren't you?" Her voice was angry.

 But the man said, "You can wave as you go by." He was laughing but the set of the woman's shoulders said she did not see the funny side of it at all.

 I started thinking about my captors as people. With what my step-mother and her lawyer had told them, it would not be easy to persuade them I was not lying. I was sure my step-mother and her lawyer had hired them to find me. I pondered it all and it came into my mind who they could be. I considered it for several minutes and knew I was right.

I leaned up as far as my chains allowed and said, "I know who you two are. You're Jeff and Loretta Cruse. You're bounty hunters. Bail-bondsmen use you to find people who've jumped bail."

The woman turned, staring at me in surprise, and the man turned his head briefly to look at me too. I went on, "Using sheriff deputy's uniforms when you're transporting someone who has not been picked up on a warrant is illegal."

In the following silence, I wondered if I should not have said it. Then the man said, "You're a proper lawyer's daughter, aren't you?"

"Yes," I said. "And I'm not a druggie."

"Your mother alleges you have been using drugs and stealing her medications," the man said.

"Does she?" I said and made my voice derisive. "She's not really my mother. She's my step-mother. And I have never, ever used drugs. I'm willing to take blood tests."

"Are you?" The woman said in a tone indicating she thought I was a liar. "And I suppose you didn't steal her medications and you also didn't steal any money from her when you ran off."

"No," I said. "I told my other trustee all about it. You have a smart phone. I can give you his name and e-mail address and you can see what he says."

"Like I said, a real smart-ass," was the woman's response.

"Okay," I responded. "I dare you to send an e-mail."

She shook her head. "Your mother has already arranged for you to enter some kind of treatment center. They can sort it out."

"Will they?" I said with my voice heavy with sarcasm. "She'll have them shoot me full of drugs and keep me quiet until she has her hands safely on the money."

The woman said, "Shut up. I need to get some sleep."

We went through the drive-thru of a McDonald's in Mountain View and they pulled over into an unoccupied part of a large parking lot in front of a small Walmart and unlocked my chain so I could eat. They gave me a chicken burger, fries, and a coke. Jeff offered me a second chicken burger and I declined but asked for water. They both ate three chicken burgers with large containers of fries.

Later we stopped at a Murphy Express Gas Station in front of a Walmart in Mountain Grove. They gassed up and we went to the restroom. It was a one room affair. Loretta took me in, waited while I went, and took me back to the jeep. Two women were waiting when we came out of the restroom and I said urgently, "I'm being kidnapped."

Loretta Cruse said, "Smart mouth." She turned to the shocked women and said, "I'm a deputy sheriff and she's being transported back to California on drug and theft charges."

I could see the women believed her.

When we got back to the jeep, Loretta said, "No food next time we eat." She and Jeff took turns going to the restroom while the other one babysat me. Loretta took over driving and Jeff went to sleep.

That set the pattern for our travels. We did fast food drive-thrus and ate in empty places. They stopped every two or three hours and changed drivers. The other one always slept, or at least appeared to sleep.

After it got dark, I also slept. It was uncomfortable and I developed a crick in my neck, but I could not stay awake. We went down I-44 and the turnpikes to Oklahoma City and were going straight through to California on I-40.

I didn't get another chance to tell anyone I was being kidnapped. If anyone was near me, Loretta warned them to stand back because I was a prisoner being transported to jail. People couldn't scamper fast enough. It was almost funny how scared they were because I was still handcuffed and wearing leg irons. What could I possibly do?

It got dark again before we crossed the Colorado River into California. I had been awake most of the day but I wasn't comfortable. I began to relish the pit stops and try to do a few exercises. Loretta said, "We'll be in Bakersfield before morning."

We stopped for gas at Barstow and I didn't expect us to stop again before Bakersfield. It's only about 130 miles. But we had left I-40 and were on Highway 58. Out in the desert at a place officially called Kramer Junction, but locally known as Four Corners, is a four-way stop. As we approached it, I was asleep but woke up when Loretta, who was driving, ripped out with an obscenity. She was the one with the potty mouth, not her husband. She rolled down her window and said, "What's up, Bro?"

"Checking for drugs, ma'am. Would you pull over here, please?" The man was wearing a uniform and carrying a big gun.

"Look, I'm transporting a bail-jumper back to Bakersfield."

"Yes, ma'am. Our tip said the contraband was being transported in a jeep like yours so we need to check."

We pulled over and they had Jeff and Loretta both get out of the vehicle and produce ID. I noticed the Kern County California badges were gone. I heard them start talking but then the door of the jeep was opened and a light was put straight on me. It was too bright and I closed my eyes and turned my head. Then I heard a familiar voice say, "Dria."

I couldn't believe it. It was Forrest Hunter.

In my astonishment, I said, "What are you doing here?"

"I couldn't let a pair of eyes like yours get away, now could I?" He was smiling.

He left but returned in just a few minutes with Granny in her wheelchair. I was astonished. She grinned and wanted to know if I was okay. I wanted to know if Sue Ellen was okay. She said, "I told those people you would have never left that child alone in your car."

I asked Granny and Forrest how they found me and he grinned and said, "Second Sight." I looked at him intently and he said, "When we get you out of here, I'll tell you all about it." He said to me and Granny, "It's better if we don't do too much talking here." He took Granny back to some other vehicle.

The fuss went on and on. I knew Loretta had the keys to my chains in her pocket but the men who stopped us were not official law enforcement and Loretta was not giving them over. When the law arrived, it was a California Highway Patrol officer. He was bewildered by the situation and waited until a car arrived with two San Bernadino County sheriff's deputies before anything was done.

They undid the chain to let me out of the jeep but left the handcuffs and leg irons. When they checked, no official warrants had been issued for my arrest. My step-mother had not filed any charges against me.

I told my story with Granny to back me up and Forrest standing listening. Forrest was wearing glasses and they made him look less physical and more intellectual, sort of like a California college professor dressed in camos. They told the law officers they wanted Jeff and Loretta Cruse charged with both child endangerment and kidnapping. It turned out the two actually had some kind of official standing with the Kern County sheriff's department.

I said, "They had no arrest warrant for me. They used their badges to keep people from questioning why they had me in cuffs. That's a violation and you know it is. They knew it too. They pulled their badges off when they were being stopped."

The hassle went on long past daybreak. Eventually someone undid my cuffs and I went to the restroom accompanied by a female sheriff's deputy. Forrest brought me some food from a cafe.

Forrest Hunter's friends were a Marine Sargent and a few of his men from Camp Pendleton. It was someone Forrest had served with in the middle-east. Because of Sarge and because of Granny, the law officers were inclined to believe what Forrest said.

It took most of the day. In the end, I had to promise to appear in court when called. As they told me this, they also told Granny and I realized they thought she really was my grandmother. I kept quiet but I knew she and Forrest both knew about the misunderstanding and had let it ride. I wondered if they had even helped it along.

Before Sarge left, he came over to me and said, "Hunter says you're another one. You two should produce some really interesting children."

He walked away and I sat stunned, speechless with shock. *Whatever had made him think Forrest and I planned to have some children together?*

When we were finally released, I discovered Forrest and Granny had arrived in a small plane Forrest owned and flew. Four Corners had a small private landing strip. Forrest said, "We'll go as far as Barstow and spend the night and fly home tomorrow."

The plane was noisy and Forrest was busy so I didn't ask questions until we were dropped to a motel in Barstow. Granny had brought me clean clothes. "On faith," she said. I happily took a shower and Forrest took us to eat.

We ordered food and then I said to Forrest, "Okay. I'm dying of curiosity. How did you do it?"

The uproar over my disappearance got underway before I was carried past the Davis General Store. Glen had tried to call me to find out when I would be home. He got a Butler County sheriff's deputy. Glen told the deputy he'd be coming after Sue Ellen immediately. He also told the deputy to look in my phone and call my relatives out by Fisk. The sheriff's department was inundated with people claiming I would never have abandoned Sue Ellen, therefore it was obvious I had been abducted. My purse being found in my car was confirmation.

When Glen and Granny talked to Sue Ellen, she said I was yelling "help, help" and some "big people," a man and a woman took me away in a jeep. She said the man had no hair and a picture on his arm.

They told the sheriff's people who were doubtful about Sue Ellen being a reliable witness. Granny had said, "Remember those people driving a jeep who said they wanted to look at Dria's car. He had a shaved head and they both had tattoos. Then that night, Spot ran someone off and Dria wondered if it was them."

My photo and description went out on the evening news. The two women I had spoken to in Mountain Grove saw it. When they contacted law enforcement, they said it was the part about my eyes which got their attention. How many people had eyes like that? Also the description of my clothes was right. The information was passed on to the Butler County sheriff's department.

In the meantime, Forrest Hunter had gotten involved. Glen put Sue Ellen to bed and kept her out of sight. When Granny told Forrest about the couple in the jeep, he went out to look at my car which Glen and Granny had brought home. He found a tracking device.

He called the sheriff's department and said, "Whoever took her had a tracker on her car and we think we have a description." They told him about the possible sighting at Mountain Grove.

Forrest told Granny, "Law enforcement is too slow. I think her step-mother in Bakersfield, California is behind this. At first light, I'm taking off in the plane and going out there. Granny, will you go with me?"

While Granny slept, Forrest recruited help. Just before daylight, he had Granny aboard and they lifted off, headed west. He was meeting a friend at Four Corners where Operation Cat Eyes was going into action.

Forrest told me, "I knew as soon as Granny told me about the couple in the jeep that they had you."

"So you set up at Four Corners and stopped every jeep coming through?"

Forrest grinned. "It's a four way stop. Easy enough to pick out the right jeep – a bald man with tattoos and a woman looking like she could be law enforcement."

Granny said, "Those sheriff's people didn't much like the citizen action but they had to admit it worked."

Forrest said, "We were careful. We never said we were law enforcement and military personnel normally wear uniforms and carry guns. No one ever pointed a gun at anyone and in fact, we made sure none of the weapons were even loaded."

Later, with Granny out of earshot, I asked, "Where did your friend, Sarge, get the idea you and I had something going?"

Forrest grinned. "Don't we?" he said.

"No!" I protested.

"Well, he needed a reason for why I was in such an all-fired conniption fit to find you. Besides, I had asked you out and I'll keep asking you out until you say yes."

It was dangerous ground and I changed the subject. "Forrest, I really do thank you for coming after me. If they had carried me on to Bakersfield and that treatment center Belle had picked out, I doubt if I would have been able to get out before she managed to get her hands on my inheritance."

"Is it that much?" he asked. He could be so direct.

"Yes," I admitted but didn't want to say how much.

Forrest didn't ask.

That night after my prayers, I lay wake thinking about Forrest. I was torn. I was wildly attracted to him and equally terrified of him. In one of my fairy stories, a dragon appeared when little Mary Ellen was in serious trouble. He was not a tame dragon but a wild one. He wasn't sure what he wanted to do with Mary Ellen – breathe fire on her, eat her for lunch, or let her ride on his back. Forrest was like that dragon. He might burn me. He might eat me. Or he might take me on a delightfully magical journey.

In my fairy story, Mary Ellen made friends with the dragon and took that enchanted flight but that was a fairy story, not real life.

Chapter 8: A Friend

We landed at Forrest's place and he took Granny and I home in his jeep. Glen came to the top of the stairs and called down, "I'm putting Sue Ellen to bed."

Forrest laughed. "Am I ever going to see that child? I catch glimpses of her and all of you talk about her so I know she exists but she's always sleeping or gone when I'm here."

"She's really shy about strangers," I said.

Granny said to Forrest, "Do you want hot chocolate?"

We sat at the kitchen table drinking the chocolate and chatting idley. I wondered how long before I could get my purse and phone back from the sheriff's office. Forrest said, "Oh, I forgot. Your computer is out at my place."

"What's it doing at your place?" I asked, thinking about all those fairy stories and poems in it. But it had a password

Forrest looked at me and I knew he had caught the tension in my question. He explained they had tried to contact my trustee.

I said, "But what about the password?"

Forrest laughed. "I know someone. He gave me directions on the phone and I had everything open in just a few minutes."

I was disconcerted and Forrest was amused. He said, "Your password is only on Windows, not on your computer boot-up. Any half-way decent computer person can get around it."

I wanted to go get my computer immediately but he said, "It can wait till morning. My housekeeper comes tomorrow so if I'm not there, you can still get it. We've had long day and you two need to get to bed."

As soon as Forrest was gone, Sue Ellen came running downstairs.

She was awake long past her normal bedtime. She greeted me with all the enthusiasm she usually reserved for her daddy. Glen said, "She kept asking for you."

I told Sue Ellen, "You're a smart little girl. You told your daddy about the man with no hair and the picture on his arm taking me away in a jeep. Granny went with her friend and they caught that man."

"Wath he a bad man?" Sue Ellen asked.

I smiled. "Not really," I said. "Someone else who is very bad told that man a lot of lies."

"Thewe wath a lot of polithmen. They thaid they'd get that bad man and put him in thail," she said.

"Yes," I told her. "The policemen catch bad people and put them in jail." I held the child in my arms and wished life was that simple.

The next morning, we discussed the new project. Granny had estimates from the electrician and the plumber. She said, "The biggest expense will be redoing the wiring. But even for the bed and breakfast, it needs to be done. The electrician said it had been well done when it was installed back in the 40's just after the war but he was surprised it still worked. He showed me places and declared it was a major fire risk and should all be replaced."

The plumber had recommended keeping the old heating system. He said it looked like it was in good shape and was fairly economical to run. This fall he would come back and turn it on and inspect it.

The older Amish couple turned up with Samuel and Sofie. Samuel and his father were working on the roof. They had heard I was back and wanted to hear all about it.

In the old restaurant, I found the Amish men had chalked out a proposed layout for the booths. They also had a sketch of a layout for a mezzanine. It would be on the level of the hotel bedrooms and would be reached by the old stairway already in place. It would be over only half the old restaurant, leaving the outside wall with its long windows to give light and a sense of spaciousness. Mr. Miller said, "It would not be difficult to build. We checked in the basement to see where the support pillars are located and it works out well. We suggest that instead of solid walls, use a framework between the booths with chicken wire on it. It's lighter and cheaper than installing solid walls and in the future, if someone wants to do something different, it can easily be taken down. The sellers can hang pictures and other things on the chicken wire more easily than on a solid wall.

I told Granny and Glen we needed more research on running the business. We talked about the computer being used in Country Bumpkins. I suggested taking Sue Ellen and visiting several businesses to see what I could find out.

Granny thought her ankle was ready to come out of its cocoon and insisted on unwrapping it. She said, "It isn't ready to be walked on really but it needs some exercise." She continued to use the walker and wheelchair but was working her foot up and down when she sat.

Since Sofie and her mother were there, I asked them to take care of Sue Ellen while I went after my computer. I arrived at a gate and could see nothing but trees and a sign saying "Dragon Hold." It was an odd name. I pushed a button and a woman's voice said, "Hello." I said who I was and the gate opened. I drove through and watched it close itself behind me.

The evening before, I had only caught a glimpse of Forrest's house through the woods. Now I paused in the road before it and stared. It was half hidden in the trees but I could see it was one of those modern log houses. However, it didn't look like the standard production. It was big and spilled down a hillside, nestled in the trees. It was convoluted with staggered levels, odd balconies, and lots of windows. It looked interesting. I suddenly knew I was going to love it.

I did. The front porch had rustic looking chairs. I rang the bell and was startled when it was answered by Gloria's mother. She was Forrest's part-time housekeeper. She told me, "Forrest said you were coming by. He's up in his study." She sent me up an open stairway and I looked as I climbed at a high-ceilinged living room with a massive stone fireplace. The furniture was wood with warm brown leather and bright pillows in an American Indian looking pattern. On one wall was a Navajo rug. The floor was polished wood. I saw odd shaped wooden lamps and American Indian pottery.

I reached the top of the stairs and Forrest called, "In here." The door was standing open.

His study was an open room with book shelves and wide windows and a balcony over-looking trees with the landing strip and hanger for his plane in the distance.

He said, "Come on in. Have a seat."

He had been typing on a computer but he swiveled his chair around and waved at a comfortable looking leather chair facing him. He had been wearing his glasses but he took them off and looked at me intently. I floundered, unable to think of anything to say.

He smiled and said, "Sometimes I do things I shouldn't." His expression became mischievous. "I took a peek in your computer," he confessed, "and then I was fascinated." He paused and looked at me solemnly. "I hope you're not really mad," he said. "I couldn't resist."

"You read them," I said.

"You should publish," he responded.

"Publish what?" I asked, wondering how much he had read.

"The Mary Ellen stories and the poetry both, although poetry with rhyme is out of fashion just now."

"You read it all," I said and felt dismayed. I had never written for others to read. My writing was for me, my own way of dealing with a reality which was sometimes difficult.

"I'm sorry," he said. "I didn't read your journal but the stories and the poetry, I couldn't resist. I can see that you . . . " He trailed off and was silent.

I said, "No one's ever read any of it before."

"It's your own private world," he said.

"Yes," I said, looking away and focusing on a framed print on his wall, "my own private retreat where I'm safe and can say what I really feel."

"Dria," he said softly, "you can always say how you really feel to me."

I looked at him. "I don't really know you."

"We can easily fix that," he said.

"I don't know," I said, standing up, and moving to pick up my computer lying on his desk in front of a photo of a couple with a child. I knew it was Forrest with his wife and son.

He asked, "Dria, are you afraid of me?"

"A little," I admitted and stopped. He just looked at me. Without forethought, I said, "Granny described you as a odd soul."

He laughed.

Then something about the print at which I had been staring jumped into my mind and I looked at it again. It was an enlargement of the picture on the jacket of a book I had read and really liked. The book was one in a series of fantasy adventure books which I had liked so well I had bought all of them and read them through several times. My eyes moved to another print. It was the picture on the cover of another book in the series. I looked around the room. They were all there, all six of them arranged in sequence but beyond them was a seventh print. I walked over and looked. It was clearly the next one in the series but I had never seen it before. The series had only had six books.

Then I saw the books on a shelf, all six in a row. They were written by someone called Jay Hunter. It sizzled through me like an electric shock.

I looked at Forrest and said, "You're Jay Hunter."

I saw the look on his face. He was completely disconcerted.

We were both as still as statues, unmoving, caught in one of those crazy moments where neither of you know what to say.

Finally he gently shook his head and said, "I've probably had more than two hundred people see this room and you're the first person who recognized the pictures."

"They aren't prints, are they? They're the illustrator's original work."

He sighed. "My wife," he said.

And suddenly I saw it all – the love, the grief, the loss, the empty place in his life.

I sat back down. We were quiet and then Forrest said, "Some days I think I've recovered and then other days . . ." He spread his hands in a helpless gesture and in his eyes, I saw tears.

Again there was a long silence while Forrest's sadness filled the room. Finally he looked at me and said, "I'm sorry."

I looked at him and said, "Don't apologize for your grief. Grief is supposed to be shared."

Forrest said, "Dria, will you be my friend?"

I smiled at him. "I've read your stories about the Orphan Arthur through at least six times. Maybe I already know you."

He smiled. "I loved your Mary Ellen stories. I was serious about publishing. I think others would love them too."

I looked again at the seventh illustration. He saw my glance and said, "When Ella was shot, she had just finished that one. I had the book written and was ready to start editing. I never published it."

I said, "Publish it as a memorial to Ella."

He was looking at the painting, "And our son, Jay. He was the model for her drawings of Arthur."

Then I remembered one of the things which had intrigued me about the books was the eyes of the orphan boy, Arthur. He had ringed eyes. They were Forrest's eyes. And Sue Ellen's. My eyes went back to the photo on Forrest's desk. The woman was blonde and blue-eyed but the boy looked like Sue Ellen. Then I saw another photo of just the woman. She was pretty.

I sighed. "I need to get back to the store. I'm supposed to be looking after Sue Ellen."

We exchanged phone numbers and as I was leaving he said to me, "Friends?"

I smiled at him and held out my hand for a handshake. "Friends," I said.

On my way home, I remembered the Orphan Arthur books had sketches scattered through them which is common in older books but not in those published in recent years. The artist was Ella Hunter. His wife had illustrated his books.

I was glad Forrest had not found my sketchbooks. I was not nearly the artist his wife had been but he might very well have found the co-incidence painful. It was enough of a co-incidence that Forrest and I had both written stories in which the main character was an orphan. I would never, ever have chosen to show my stories to the author of the Orphan Arthur series. I was glad he did not think I was copy-catting in any way but then our stories were quite different.

I speculated on why no one seemed to know that Forrest was the author, Jay Hunter. Maybe it was a secret, so back home at the store, I said nothing about it.

Chapter 9: Confession

The rest of Thursday was quietly busy. Sue Ellen wanted to stay with me and I was surprised at how strongly she seemed to be attached to me. But then I had spent a lot of time with her and given her a lot of attention. Glen said, "I think all children want a mother."

I smiled at him and said, "And a daddy."

I thought about my Mary Ellen stories. Mary Ellen lived in an orphanage run by nuns. Her fairy and other magical friends could only be seen by her. One of her biggest desires was parents.

We decided that Friday, I would take Sue Ellen and go investigate antique malls and flea markets. After some discussion, we asked Gloria if she would like to go with me. Everyone was a little insecure about me going anywhere with only Sue Ellen.

I discovered I had been located through my car insurance agent. Belle Davis might have another try but I didn't think so.

We went first back to Country Bumpkins and the owner was present. When he found out who I was, he expressed his shock over having someone kidnapped out of his parking lot. He said the day it happened, someone had noticed Sue Ellen right away. They had come into the market indignant, looking for the miscreant who had left such a small child alone in a car in the summer sun. One of the women went out to look, recognized Sue Ellen, found the car door unlocked, and saw my purse. They called the sheriff's office.

He showed me the computer program they used and gave me a lot of helpful information. He even told me he had a few vendors who had booths in several places and he would ask if they were interested in a place up the other side of Ellsinore.

We made the rounds of all the places. Each one had a different character. Some sold clothes and some didn't. Some had furniture and appliances. There was an incredible variety of things being offered for sale from impressive antiques to outright junk. I asked questions about booth sizes, prices, bookkeeping systems, problems with security, and choosing vendors. Only one person didn't want to give me information and some were more helpful than others. All of them asked where our proposed business would be located. I asked if they worried about competition and got answers from a straight "yes" to "the more, the merrier." The latter said cheerfully, "None of us will have exactly the same things."

We headed home with Sue Ellen asleep. Gloria and I had talked off and on all day. Her mother was encouraging her to get contacts. I told her, "Becoming an adult is a little scary. I don't mind if you ask me for advice but I'm still figuring some of it out myself."

I asked her if she had any idea what she wanted to do in the future. She didn't. I told her about helping my father and deciding I did not want to be a paralegal or a lawyer. Then I worked in a daycare and loved it so I got a certificate and became a pre-school teacher. "What do you really enjoy?" I asked her.

Her answer was animals. They had a dog, some cats, and a lot of cattle but she also liked horses and other animals. I asked about their veterinarian. He and his wife had an office in Van Buren. I suggested she find out if they ever hired teenagers to help out. "They might have a trainee program where they don't pay you much but you would be learning things and getting experience."

Back home, Sue Ellen greeted her father with enthusiasm and he took her out to play while Granny and I did the store. Granny said, "It's weird. All this with you getting kidnapped has led to more people coming into the store. We've always had some customers who don't want to go even as far as Ellsinore and others run in here for bits and pieces but there were other people here in the area who never came here. Now a number of them have stopped in checking the place out.

It's a little strange."

I talked to Granny about what I had learned from all the antique and flea market operators. I told her, "All of the stores were different. Some were much more flea markets while others were more antiques and collectibles. Some had handcrafts. All of them had some furniture but some more than others. Some even had used appliances. Some didn't sell clothes but one place had a booth with hospital scrubs and a large booth selling only jeans. Some places told me they were careful about choosing their vendors and others said it just depended on if they had an empty booth when someone asked. Another issue I asked about was shoplifting. Three places had surveillance cameras. The others all said they weren't losing that much but I wondered if they were making excuses for not installing any surveillance. The Country Bumpkins man said he didn't have it when he first opened but installed it because of losses. I'm going to do some research on surveillance systems, how they work, prices, and so on."

Granny showed me the layout the Amish men had suggested. The general store and the old hotel dining room were the same size, 48 feet wide and 108 feet long, which is big. These two rooms already had pillars, eight in a row down the middle of each room, supporting their ceilings. About half the shelves in the general store were empty. It was a massive stone building, about 100 feet wide and about 150 feet long. The Amish men had suggested making most of the booths 10 feet by 12 feet. They said this would put the weight where the pillars in the basement were located and fit with the already existing support pillars. The mezzanine would cover half the old restaurant room, ending in the middle at the pillars already in place. The layout they suggested would create on the main floor 28 booths which were 10 feet by 12 feet, 3 booths 10 feet by 8 feet, and 1 booth only 6 feet by 10 feet. The one small booth was necessitated by the location of doors going into the general store side of the building. Opening up those doors would allow the general store customers easy access to the restrooms located under the stairs at the back of the old restaurant. That would be 32 booths. If we added the mezzanine, it would create 15 booths 10 feet by 12 feet and 1 booth 10 feet by 8 feet. That would total 48 booths. Also at the front of the store where the counter would be located, they could put 3 more booths which were 8 feet by 10 feet or we could think of other ways to use the space. Maybe we wanted an area with a table and coffee and snacks for tired shoppers to rest.

The men recommended strengthening the pillars for the mezzanine all the way up to the ceiling. They said, "That attic could be put to use. You'd need to add fire escapes but it's basically a solid building."

Granny said the electrician told her this layout was totally feasible for wiring and he suggested installing the needed breaker switches and some lines which would allow the attic and cellar to be wired in the future, if desired. The added cost would be minimal if it was done now with the other wiring.

I could tell Granny was excited about the project. She said, "The Amish have even asked about helping to run the business. In fact they've ask me about selling stuff in the store now and I'm going to do it. All those empty shelves can be put to use."

That evening after Sue Ellen was in bed, I got the Orphan Arthur books out of the box where they were packed. The series was set in a mythical kingdom called Woodsdale. The culture of the kingdom was medieval with knights and kings and queens and all the other levels of medieval society. The orphan boy, Arthur, had a job which was to protect and help look after a set of twins, a boy and a girl, who were slow-minded but obedient and tried very hard to learn things. The sketches in the books revealed them clearly to be Down Syndrome. The twins were called George and Georgana and their mother was dead. Arthur had been told they were being raised in secret because George was the future king of Woodsdale. As a part of keeping this secret, George and Georgana did not know they were royalty and were not to be told.

The twins and everyone else had been told George and Georgana were the grandchildren of the Lord in whose castle they lived. This

Lord had once had a son who went off to war and did not return. The babies had been born after he left. Their mother was supposed to have been a slow-minded servant girl who died when they were born.

Arthur was diligent about his job but it was not an easy one. The sequence of stories followed the children from about age 5 up to 15. I loved the stories. They were filled with compassion and insight and Arthur's struggle to do what was right. A wise old priest advised Arthur and a wicked witch searched for the king's heir, wanting to kill him. There were unicorns and dragons and other mythical creatures.

Through it all was Arthur's steadfast faith in God. It was presented in the fashion of the faith of medieval knights but it was a consistent part of the stories. I think it was this aspect of the tales which brought about their inclusion in the library of my Catholic school. That library included only fiction which presented good Christian standards.

The first time I came across the Arthur stories, I had seen the similarities to my Mary Ellen stories but I thought the Arthur stories were much deeper and better written. My stories were all short stories, not novels like the Arthur stories. They were set in modern American but with the addition of fantasy. Each time Mary Ellen went off on an adventure, she returned to her orphanage and promised the nuns to be good. She never told them what happened and they found her an exasperating child who frightened them by disappearing from time to time – but they loved her.

I started reading the Arthur stories through again with the added knowledge of who wrote them. I occurred to me that Forrest had written them for his son.

Saturday we were outside when Sue Ellen started drawing in the dirt with a stick and I saw she had made S U 3 E ll c N. I was quite impressed. For a 3-year-old, it was brilliant. I learned Sofie had been teaching her. I had already decided Sue Ellen was brighter than the average child her age. It was her speech which hid that. I helped her correct her writing and started working with her on her 's' sound. I soon had her running around going 's-s-s-s-s-s-s' like a bumble bee.

It was funny and Granny laughed and encouraged her to do it for her daddy. We got her to practice saying "Sue Ellen" over and over and praised her for her performance.

Granny was making good progress with her ankle and she was cautiously practicing walking a few steps at a time. Her ribs were actually more of a problem than the ankle.

That evening when Sue Ellen was in bed, we discussed the new project. Granny said, "In some ways, it's been like a run-away. Once the idea was proposed, everyone has been sort of pushing it along. I thought we could handle the bed and breakfast with only a part-time cleaning woman but once the antique store idea got going, they have all been enthusiastic. Even for the bed and breakfast, the plumbing and wiring would need to be updated and the cost of adding the antique mall is not much more. I've been doing some arithmetic and an antique mall should be a good money maker, better than a bed and breakfast. We would need someone all the time and really we should have two people if we are going to prevent shoplifting. If a surveillance system is not more expensive than hiring someone full-time for a year, then we probably should do it."

Granny's antique cash register had come home working better than before its baptism with cooking oil but the adding machine Granny had been using had to be replaced. Glen had found a bookkeeping program and Granny was learning to use a computer. She loved the fact that the program did sums instantly and accurately.

Forrest was coming again to guard the place while we went to church on Sunday morning. We juggled it nicely so he didn't see Sue Ellen but he said he wanted to talk to me about publishing my writing. Granny was out of earshot and I said, "I don't want to talk about it around Granny or Glen."

He smiled. "I'll take you out to dinner."

"Okay," I said.

Today's scheduled preacher was another seminary student. His sermon was good but he read it off a paper and the language made me wonder if he took it out of a printed volume of sermons. For once, I was ignored, which was fine with me, and Gloria's family took him home for dinner. I had the idea they had gotten a rather dull stick but judging a book by it's cover sometimes gives you a surprise.

At home, Glen took Sue Ellen into the back door of the old kitchen on the other side of the building. We came in and Forrest shut down his computer. He said, "Where's Glen?"

"Sue Ellen left some toys in the other side of the building yesterday," I said, which was true, "and they've gone to retrieve them. Are you ready to go?"

Out in Forrest's jeep, he headed toward Van Buren. "Does Glen have something against me?" he asked.

I considered. He had clearly picked up on something. It was better to provide a reason. "I got the idea that maybe you and Pam had something going before he married her."

He slammed on his brakes and pulled over onto the shoulder.

"What has Pam said?" he demanded.

"I've never actually met Pam," I said. "I just kind of picked up the idea that Glen thinks that. Maybe I'm wrong."

He drew in a deep breath and sighed. " 'Your sins will always find you out,' " he quoted. He shook his head. "When Ella was lying in the hospital in a coma, I started drinking. I was half crazy with grief but it's no excuse. I did some really stupid things and Pam was undoubtedly the stupidest."

I tried frantically to think of something tactful to say but couldn't. In the silence, Forrest continued, "She even claimed she was pregnant and wanted me to give her money for an abortion. I told her if she was really pregnant, then I wanted to accompany her to a doctor for confirmation. I'd pay her medical bills and I would keep the baby but I would not pay for an abortion. Then she up and married Glen so it was his baby."

He paused and then said, "She tried to come around after she and Glen moved up here last spring and I wouldn't let her on my place.

Then Ray brought her with him that day they vandalized the store. I told them she couldn't come into the house and I wouldn't talk to her. Ray asked to borrow my jeep. He told me some cock-and-bull story about Pam trying to reconcile with Glen. They said they were going to wait outside the church and if Glen saw Ray's car outside, then he would not come out to talk."

He looked at me and said, "After Pam, I quit drinking and I promised myself I was never going to kiss another woman unless I was going to marry her."

"I guess that's one way to keep yourself out of trouble," I said and then instantly wondered if I sounded flippant.

But Forrest threw back his head and laughed. He said, "Dinner and talk but no kissing. Is that okay?"

"Very okay," I answered. Just thinking about him kissing me gave me the shivers. I realized I was a coward. I did not want to risk getting too close to the fire.

He said, "Dria, what is it about you that makes me feel it's okay to bare my soul?"

"I don't know," I told him, "but you don't seem like the sort of person who normally tells lies."

"No," he said, "but there's a lot of space between not lying and telling all." I looked at him and he was smiling and I suddenly felt guilty about hiding Sue Ellen. If someone just talked to him, would he understand?

We passed Van Buren and crossed the Current River. I wondered where we were going but saw more town on the other side of the river. A sign with an arrow said "Big Spring 4 Miles" and we took the turn. He took me to a lodge with a dining room. It was constructed of logs and stone and Forrest told me it had been built during the Depression by the Civilian Conservation Corps. He said, "We'll eat and then look at the spring."

When we had ordered, I asked, "Are you not telling anyone you wrote the Orphan Arthur stories?"

He begin running his hand through his hair. It was a gesture I come to recognize as an indication of agitation. He had been doing it in the jeep as he talked about Pam. He said, "It's never been strictly a secret. A few people know, of course, but we never talk about it."

"It's more like private information."

"Yes," he said. "I really wouldn't mind if Granny knew but she wouldn't understand about not telling the world."

"I know," I said. "It's like my Mary Ellen stories."

He smiled. "Mary Ellen enchanted me."

"I wrote the first one when I was 10. I had the measles and they didn't want me back at school for two weeks. I was bored and I was drawing a fairy and my Grandmother said why didn't I write a story about a little girl who had a fairy for a friend."

"I was serious about publishing," he said. "I hold papers for a publishing company. We actually publish through something called CreateSpace but we have our own label."

As Forrest and I talked, I saw he really was totally serious about publishing my stories. Then he asked, "Do you still draw?" Again I thought how direct he was.

"Sometimes," I admitted, "but nothing like your wife. I just sketch and use colored pencils."

"Will you let me see them?" he asked.

I shrugged. "They aren't that good."

"I still would like to see them," he said.

Forrest asked if I would enjoy a hike and we walked from the Lodge to the spring. When we crossed a bridge from which the spring was visible, we stopped to look and I said, "My goodness! It's like a river coming out of the bluff!"

As we walked to the spring, I discovered he knew the history of the area, the Civilian Conservation Corps, and the forming of the Ozark National Scenic Riverways Park. We discussed it all off and on between talking about the spring and everything we were seeing. Forrest knew all the plants and trees by name. We had approached the spring by way of a mowed area with a pavilion and a playground. I made a note to myself to bring Sue Ellen. We admired the spring which was lovely and then took a path which ran under the bluffs down the other side of the spring stream. He said, "I grew up coming here. This a wildlife refuge but this time of day, the deer retreat into the woods."

On the way home, I called Glen and warned him that we were coming. When we arrived, I saw his SUV was gone. Forrest said, "I want to see your drawings but if you don't want to show Granny, we can do it some other time."

"Yes, please," I answered.

He came in and Granny gave him coffee and cake. He admired the progress she was making with her ankle. We started discussing the new project again and along the way, the cellar was mentioned. He had not seen the cellar. Granny told me to go show him the cellar and the attic.

He inspected the pillars and the two foot wide stone wall down the center supporting the upper floors and said, "I see what they mean about a good solid building." Each stone pillar was about 2 feet by 2 feet and all of them appeared to be in good shape. Forrest said, "If there is enough demand in the future, this could be turned into selling space."

As he was looking at the attic, I told him about it's use in the past as a dormitory for lumberjacks. He said, "You could turn it into a youth hostel. Make a hall down the middle here where the stairs come up. One side could be for girls and one for boys. Here in the middle, you put coin operated lockers for storing backpacks and luggage. Out back by the outhouse, you build a shower house."

I said, "What about the young people waking everyone up going up and down the stairs to the toilets during the night? I'm not sure we could install toilets up here."

Forrest laughed. "You're right. Maybe more selling space would be a better idea."

Forrest asked when he could see my drawings and I saw he was not going to drop it. I said, "I don't want to drag them out in front of

Granny."

"Bring them to my place," he said. "You can bring Sue Ellen along. I like children."

I said, "We'll see. I'll call you."

When he was gone, I called Glen and told him the coast was clear.

Then I reflected that helter-skelter with no forethought or intention, I was now launched on a project to become a published author. I was scared. Again it was like Mary Ellen's wild dragon. I might get burned. I might get eaten. Or it might turn out to be an exciting, fascinating adventure.

Granny asked, "Did you have a good time?"

I said, "You know you want every detail." She grinned. I said, "He took me to eat at the lodge at Big Spring. I hadn't seen the spring before. It's a beautiful place."

Granny nodded. "Are you going out with him again?"

I said, "It wasn't really like that. I've done a little writing and because he's published those books you sell in the store, he knows about publishing. That's mostly what we talked about."

Granny said, "I'm old enough to know when a man is interested in a woman and and he's interested in you."

Mostly as something less scary to discuss, I asked, "How old is he?"

"Thirty-two," she answered. "You're twenty and that's a twelve year gap but it's not necessarily too much. My father was twenty years older than my mother. His first wife died and he married again and had a second family. They were happy together."

"How long has Forrest lived out there?" I asked, knowing Granny would know where I meant.

"I tried to count up," Granny said. "He and his wife started building that beautiful house nine or ten years ago. The boy was maybe 3 then. He'd just gotten out of the military. Local gossip said he had money. His wife was an artist. She had a studio at the top of the house, I heard, and people came and went, other artists and so on. At first, he was going to college to get a teaching credential and then he was hired over at Van Buren to teach in the high school. But he only taught one year before the boy was killed and his wife was laying in the hospital in a coma. They had always come to church pretty regular." Granny paused and then said, "Since the shooting, Forrest has never been in the church again."

Then she sighed, "It was like without his wife and son, he lost himself. He drank and run with bad company. Then Ella died and he quit drinking and pulled himself together." She shook her head. "I don't know how Sue Ellen happened but Forrest is basically a good man."

I went to bed that night and lay awake thinking about Forrest. I had planned not to get anywhere near him but it kept happening. His rescuing me when I was kidnapped was amazing and I could not help seeing him as a kind of hero.

His confession about Pam did not scare me off and I wondered why. I had never admired people who had sexual affairs. I had always felt like it showed low standards and lack of integrity. But I didn't feel that way about Forrest. Maybe it was his free confession of sin. I thought about it. Also about his resolve to never again kiss a woman he didn't intend to marry.

I thought about repentance. I remembered my Christian teaching. Repentance is not just admitting guilt. It's turning around and going the other way. It sounded like that is what Forrest had done.

I started praying for Forrest and fell asleep in the middle.

Chapter 10: My Trustee

On Monday morning, I asked Granny if she had really decided about the bed and breakfast. I told her if they didn't really need me here, I could go stay with Cousin Marie.

Granny said, "We really like having you here. Yesterday afternoon we heard Ray and Pam were arrested over at Branson. Glen is checking today to see if it's true. If it is, then he's going to see about getting a divorce. If she's in jail, he should get custody of Sue Ellen."

Since Sue Ellen had started learning to write so easily, I wondered if she was ready to start learning to read. I got her copy of *Green Eggs and Ham* which is one of her favorites and sat her beside me and pointed to each word as I read it. I did each page three times, encouraging her to read it with me.

Then we went out to pick the garden. Glen come out in a little while to help, leaving Granny to watch the store. I talked to him about Sue Ellen leaning to write so easily and I was trying reading with her.

He had checked and both Pam and Ray really were in jail. Then he asked, "Did you enjoy going out with Forrest?"

I shrugged and told him what I told Granny, that had done a little writing and was talking to Forrest about publishing. He said, "I've gotten the idea Forrest is interested in you."

I said, "Granny thinks so but all he's really said is I have an interesting mind. That's not romantic."

Glen shifted, looked a little nervous, and then said, "You're so good with Sue Ellen. You're the kind of woman I should have married." I looked at him and he looked at me. I knew if he were free, he would be asking me out, and more seriously, asking me to marry him.

He went back into the store with the produce we had picked and Sue Ellen was busy with her play house under the pecan tree. I thought about it. Glen was a good man and he deserved a good wife. Being married to him would mean a solid, secure life. And I loved Sue Ellen.

The Amish arrived with stuff for the store. It was jars of things like honey and relish. They also had brought some produce as they knew Granny sold it in the store. The older Amish man, John Miller, was going with Glen to check on availability and prices of what they needed for building the booths. These Amish didn't use modern vehicles but seemed to have no objections to riding in one. They left, taking Sue Ellen with them, and the women started arranging jars on shelves.

It was a perfect time to take my drawings out to Forrest. He was persistent and I might as well get it over with. Once he saw them, he would see I wasn't really a good artist. I just told Granny I needed to do something and would be gone about an hour.

When I saw the gate, it occurred to me Forrest might not be home. I didn't have his number with me. I could just leave my folder. That might be easier but what about the gate? When I pushed the button, at first no one responded and then the gate opened. At the house, I rang the bell and waited. Forrest appeared from somewhere outside. I said, "I should have phoned first but I didn't think of it until I was on my way."

He smiled and invited me in, saying, "Welcome to Dragon Hold."

"It's the name of the castle in the Orphan Arthur books."

He sighed. "Jay named it."

I had hit a nerve again. "I'm sorry," I said. And as a diversion added, "I've brought my drawings. If you're busy, I can just leave them. You'll see they aren't very good."

We went up to his study and he laid them out on a table, looking at them one by one. I had brought only the ones for my Mary Ellen stories. I resisted the urge to chatter.

Finally he said, "Your Mary Ellen stories are aimed at the 8 to 12 year old age group. These drawings are perfect. If they were too . . ."

he paused and then went on, "if they were too technically slick, they wouldn't fit the feel of your stories nearly as well."

He looked at me and smiled.

We discussed formatting my stories for printing. He said it was one of the most time consuming parts of the process and it would save a lot of expense if I did it myself. He showed me in his computer what he meant and jotted down some directions. He said I could call him any time if I needed help.

As we were going back down the stairs, I said, "I love your house."

He said, "I thought about moving after Ella died but somehow by staying, I've kept a part of her."

"Memories," I said. "Someone said to me once that as long as someone is remembered, they are not truly gone."

He nodded and said, "And I vowed to never again go anywhere without my gun."

I had noticed he was wearing it even in his own house. I wanted to ask if a gun would have prevented what happened to his wife and son but it was too painful of a question. However, it was like he had heard my thought. He said, "We were in a restaurant in Springfield. I had taken Jay to the restroom to wash our hands. He went out ahead of me and then as I came out, I heard a shot fired. I looked and a man had shot a woman who was lying on the floor. He was standing with a gun in his hand and my son was running across the room to his mother. She stood up and just as Jay reached her, the man fired. He hit Jay and it went through him to Ella. They fell to the floor and the man walked over and put another bullet in Ella's head. In the time that Jay was running to Ella, I think I could have taken him out if I'd had a gun. And I certainly could have gotten him before he put that bullet in Ella's head."

I stood perfectly still, feeling shock and his grief. After a brief silence, he moved and I said, "Forrest, life is full of *if onlys*. I think you being so quick to come after me when those bounty hunters had me is because of your family's deaths. Maybe you'll save the lives of people in the future because of it."

He looked at me and said, "You think like Granny – everything works out for the best in the long run." He shook his head. "I wish I could believe it."

Back at the general store, I found someone waiting for me. My absent trustee had appeared. He was examining the hardware section in the store, which tended to fascinate male tourists.

We had not gotten any answer to our e-mails, neither the ones I sent nor the one Forrest wrote. My trustee was Dr. Thomas Goodwin, a widower, whose friendship with my father went back to their college days together. His doctorate was in theology and he was professor at a Christian university called Vanguard in Costa Mesa, California.

I looked at him and cried, "Uncle Tom!" and moved to give him a hug. Remembering my manners, I asked if he had met the ladies in the store. He hadn't. "I want you to meet Mrs. Susan Davis, Mrs. John Miller, and her daughter, Miss Sofia Miller. I call Mrs. Davis 'Granny' and she is the proprietor of this establishment."

Uncle Tom was a big bear of a man with a neat goatee and black rimmed glasses. I said, "This is Dr. Thomas Goodwin who was a dear friend of my father's. He's a theology professor, not a medical doctor."

Uncle Tom was smiling, "The same little Dria, always so neat and mannerly."

"Come in the back," I invited, "and we can talk."

I offered him coffee, remembering he was an avid consumer. I had questions but I decided to let him ask his first. He said, "I got all those e-mails in one batch. I had been on a tour to the backside of Morocco. I made a couple of phone calls and flew home. I've filed charges against your step-mother and Jake Carson both. Also Jeff and Loretta Cruse. I've engaged a lawyer, T. John Eddingham, and we're suing all of them on your behalf. Also Jake Carson is blocked from doing anything with your father's estate."

"Wow," I said. T. John Eddingham was the biggest name in Bakersfield for lawsuits.

"T. John says we can almost certainly work a deal in which Jake Carson resigns his position as your trustee. He and Belle would have to pay back into your estate what they have managed to wangle out of it already. I am fairly sure they have forged my signature which will provoke more charges."

"Wow," I said again.

"And Jeff and Loretta Cruse are willing to go public with the whole scheme."

"They knew it was a scheme?" I asked.

"They say they didn't and I'm inclined to believe them. They are embarrassed over being duped but I told them if they provided the right kind of publicity at the right time, we'd get the charges against them dropped."

"Can you do that?"

"You were the victim. If you withdraw your complaint, they will be dropped."

"I didn't know that," I said.

"Actually Jeff Cruse says he was having doubts and was thinking maybe they ought to do a little checking once they got you to Bakersfield."

"So he did think I might be telling the truth?"

Uncle Tom smiled at me. "What he said was they had picked up druggies before and he said you didn't have the smell. I asked him what he meant and he said it was little things. He said you slept at night like a normal person and were awake in the day. He said you weren't a picky eater and every druggie they had ever picked up either wouldn't eat or insisted on certain things. He said you just ate whatever they gave you and didn't complain. He said all druggies are whiners and you weren't."

I had to laugh. Jeff Cruse undoubtedly had it pegged. No druggie would have thought of all those little things giving them away.

"Now," he said, "I want to hear all about this old lady who got some Marines to rescue you. Was that her out there?"

"Yes," I said. "She's great, isn't she?" So I told him all about it, about Granny, about Forrest Hunter, and about his Marine Sargent buddy.

When I finished, he said, "Wow," echoing my earlier comment.

I got up to get him more coffee and Sue Ellen came flying through the door. Glen was home. She stopped and looked at Tom Goodwin intently. I said, "Sue Ellen, this is my Uncle Tom come to visit me." To Tom, I said, "This is Sue Ellen Davis."

Sue Ellen unfroze and said to Tom, "Do you know how to wead?"

He nodded solemnly and said, "Yes. It's fun."

She said, "I juss' leawned. I come to get my book and ssow Misstah Millah." I smiled. She was buzzing her s's nicely.

She took her book and left and Uncle Tom said, "Can she really?"

I said, "I just started trying to teach her. We've gone through *Green Eggs and Ham* several times. She may have it memorized."

Uncle Tom regarded me seriously and said, "Your step-mother, Belle, gave your dad a hard time. He never said much about it but I could tell."

I shrugged. "He never really complained but then I didn't either. I think we both just tried to avoid her as much as possible. I could do that easier than he could."

"I think it would be a good idea to appoint more trustees for you. I know it's just until next April but if I were a dishonest man, I could make off with it all before then and disappear into the wide blue yonder."

"Uncle Tom, you would never do that."

"Yes, but appointing other trustees lessens my work load and protects me from accusations."

"Who do you suggest?" I asked.

"Your father had talked to Justin Schwartz about being a trustee but had never done the necessary paperwork."

Justin Schwartz was another lawyer and he and my dad had been good friends before Dad married Belle. Belle had done her best to push him out of Dad's life but I knew Dad had continued to lunch with him often. I nodded. "Yes," I agreed.

"I considered getting him to handle your legal work but he suggested Eddingham. He said T. John has more punch."

"Yes, and if he becomes a trustee, then you would need someone else for the lawsuit."

"For a third trustee, how about that man Granny got to help her, the one who got the Marines involved?"

"Forrest Hunter," I said. "Maybe not him."

"Why not?" Uncle Tom asked.

I sorted through what I should say. "He's asked me out. Granny thinks he's romantically interested in me although he hasn't said anything, but if he were, it would be a conflict of interest."

Uncle Tom nodded. "Might be better for him not to know how much you're worth."

"Exactly," I said, although I had not really thought of it that way. "Also he's a bit of a rebel. Carries a gun all the time and is very anti-government."

Uncle Tom nodded. "Just who you need if you get kidnapped but maybe not the best choice for a trustee. How about Granny herself?"

In the end, she was who we decided to ask and Uncle Tom produced some papers to be signed. He had come prepared. I asked him why he hadn't phoned me. He said, "At the same time I got your e-mails, I got e-mails from Belle and from Jake Carson. I made phone calls and learned Belle had told the police you were using drugs, had stolen medications from her, and had stolen some money and then vanished. I immediately flew home. I knew it didn't sound like you but I thought maybe grief and stress had driven you to drugs or maybe you had gotten into bad company. I wanted to see for myself what was going on."

Uncle Tom stayed for dinner and he stayed overnight. Uncle Tom was interested in the antique mall project and we discussed it with him. He liked the way Granny could lay things out for him clearly, knowing figures and potential income.

He stood in the door looking at the old restaurant space and said, "It even had ceiling fans!"

I said, "Yes, and most of them still work but the electrician said we should replace them. He said these old ones use too much electricity."

Sue Ellen read her book for him. She had it all memorized but I knew early readers all started that way. I would take her through the book again several times having her point to each word as she said it. Then I would start on another book. But only if she found it fun. I wasn't going to push her.

Uncle Tom finally asked me about Forrest Hunter. He wanted to know if I found him romantically interesting. I said, "I find him very attractive but also he scares me a little. He's 32. His son was killed in a shooting incident five years ago and his wife was critically injured. She lay in a coma for two years before dying. He carries a gun all the time because he thinks he could have saved them if he had had it when they were shot. He runs survival training courses. There's a poster for his next one in the store."

"And he asked you out."

I smiled. "He said I had an interesting mind and would I have dinner with him? That's not very romantic."

Uncle Tom laughed but then said, "No, but in some ways, it has more potential for a long term relationship. How many divorces have I seen because one party was bored with the other one?"

Then he said, "You've also got another one."

"Another what?" I asked.

"Sue Ellen's father, Glen. His eyes follow you constantly. He's very attracted."

I sighed. "I was beginning to suspect. But he's still married to Sue Ellen's mom. She's in jail right now so he thinks it might be a good time to file for a divorce. He wants Sue Ellen but he says her mother will only let him have her if he pays her off."

"You could pay her off."

I shook my head. "It's better if no one knows I have money. It's too much of a temptation. You did ask Granny not to tell, didn't you?"

"Yes," he answered. "I didn't tell her how much. I just said it was enough to make your step-mother and her lawyer go for it and enough to attract the wrong man if it were public knowledge. Do you think she'll tell Glen?"

"Not on purpose," I said. "And if Glen knew I really had money, it might even scare him off. Granny says he had about two hundred fifty thousand dollars when he talked his wife into marrying him. He used it to get her to marry him and he let her spend it all."

"Why?" Uncle Tom asked.

"Sue Ellen," I explained. "She told Glen it was his baby and tried to get him to pay for an abortion."

"It wasn't his baby," he said. I realized my unintentional phrasing had betrayed the truth.

"It's a secret," I said softly, urgently. "He didn't realize it until she was already 2 years old. He was totally attached to her by then. Her mother didn't care about her and it was Glen who took care of her."

"I can understand why it's better if she doesn't know but secrets like that usually come out eventually."

"Let's hope not," I said.

"It's someone awkward," Uncle Tom said.

"Very," I said.

He shook his head but said, "I admire a man who's willing to raise another man's child and call it his own."

"Yes," I said. "Glen is a good man."

The next morning I took Uncle Tom to meet Cousin Marie. We took Sue Ellen with us. Sue Ellen wanted to take her book and read it for Cousin Marie and Maggie. We had a pleasant visit with Cousin Marie and Uncle Tom reminiscing about my parents and grandmother.

On the way home, we stopped at Country Bumpkins so Uncle Tom could have a look at the sort of business Granny was considering. He bought a couple of items and talked to the proprietor. I found several books for Sue Ellen.

When we arrived home, we were unloading the car when Forrest's jeep pulled in beside the building. "Oh, no," I murmured to Uncle Tom. "I've got to get Sue Ellen out of sight." Uncle Tom followed me in the back door but I whisked Sue Ellen up the stairs and into her room.

Glen soon came up and said, "Your Uncle Tom said you thought Sue Ellen might have a little fever."

"Uncle Tom is covering for me hiding Sue Ellen," I told Glen.

"You told him," Glen said.

"Not intentionally. He guessed from how I said something. Uncle Tom is quite intelligent and he understands problems. He was quick to make an excuse for me disappearing with Sue Ellen."

Glen said, "I'll stay up here with her. You go down and talk."

Uncle Tom, Granny, and Forrest were in the store. Uncle Tom had asked about Forrest's survival training courses. I put on some coffee and went out to invite them for cake and coffee. Granny came too saying, "We can hear the bell if someone comes."

We sat at the kitchen table. Forrest said to Uncle Tom, "So you're the mysteriously absent trustee."

Uncle Tom nodded and said, "And you're the mysterious man who can talk a Marine Sargent into an unofficial operation."

Forrest asked if Tom was another lawyer and was told no, a professor of theology who taught at a Christian university. I saw the gleam in Forrest's eye and said to Uncle Tom, "Forrest dearly loves a lively theological discussion."

The topic he chose surprised me: Heaven and Hell. Forrest took the view of how could a good God sent anyone to Hell? He wanted to make an exception for sadistic murderers, rapists, and child abusers.

Uncle Tom took the stance that our eternal fate was determined by our acceptance or rejection of Jesus and his redemption. Forrest thought that was lame. He said, "So someone does all kinds of bad things and then as he's dying, just says 'Jesus, I accept you' and is into heaven."

Uncle Tom said it wasn't that simple and an hour later, I was still listening with interest. Granny and I had been in and out dealing with customers but the two men were totally focused on their discussion. Finally Forrest's phone rang and he answered it and said, "I have to go. My people are starting to arrive for the course."

He shook hands with Uncle Tom and said he'd like to talk some more sometime.

He went into the store to pick up something and Granny went with him. Uncle Tom motioned me outside. He said, "Those eyes. Couldn't be anyone else. He's an interesting man and I expect women find him very attractive."

I nodded.

He looked at me and said, "Exiting, interesting, attractive, unconventional, and possibly dangerous. I wouldn't advise getting involved with him."

"That's exactly what I told myself."

"Why did you go out with him?"

"It happened because I was helping to prevent him seeing Sue Ellen," I told him. "He took me to eat and to see Big Spring. We talked but he never said one romantic thing."

"Unless Glen takes the child and moves away from here, sooner or later he's going to see her."

"If I stay and help Granny, Glen can move back to Poplar Bluff where he teaches."

"But Sue Ellen is very attached to you and Granny."

I looked at Uncle Tom and said, "It's a mess, isn't it."

"Sin and its consequences are always messy." Uncle Tom looked sad.

Chapter 11: Family

Forrest had put out signs starting on our corner for the people arriving for his survival training course. This one was a father-and-son affair which he had never done before. I wondered if he would find it painful because of losing his own son but the sons had to be at least 12 for this course and Jay would have been younger.

It was not unusual for his participants to stop at the store on their way in. I expected them to ask for beer but Granny told me Forrest did not allow alcohol or tobacco use during his courses. I was surprised. Granny said, "He says they aren't healthy. He's real strict about what goes on during his courses. He's sent someone home more than once. If they break the rules, he just refunds their fees and tells them to leave."

Granny had decided to go ahead with the project. She said, "I'm only 62 and I'm in good health. I've got five brothers and sisters older than me and still doing fine. My father lived to be 94 and my mother 92. Herb was sick right after our son was born and the doctor said it damaged his heart. He never was really healthy after that."

The Amish men had their farm work but they said they could get help and do the work for the antique store in a couple of days. We ordered the materials and stacked them in the old restaurant. The plumber came and started adding a shower in each of the hotel bathrooms upstairs.

Business in the store was definitely up and I made a run to Poplar Bluff for stock. Sue Ellen wanted to take her books and I heard her muttering to herself in the back seat. As always I took her to McDonald's. We loaded the SUV to the roof and went home.

In the next days, we settled into a routine. All the woodwork on the building was due a coat of paint and Glen was working on it. Granny ran the store and I watched Sue Ellen, went after stock, cooked, and kept house. Granny was coaching me on cooking and I was enjoying learning. When Sunday came around, Granny said with Ray and Pam in jail, we could leave the place unguarded.

Glen filed for a divorce and when she got her papers, Pam called him. She and Ray had been working with a ring of car thieves who targeted expensive vehicles and either stripped them down for parts or shipped them out of the country. Ray was already on parole, had a history of jumping bail, and both of them were high on cocaine when arrested. Ray had injured a deputy when they were picked up and was not being granted bail. Pam's was set at a hundred thousand dollars.

Pam had a price for a divorce and custody of Sue Ellen. She wanted bail money plus twenty-five thousand dollars. She said, "You can get it from your granny."

For bail, a person normally could give a bail-bondsman a percentage to get out of jail but if the person jumped bail, the bondsman had to pay it all. I warned Glen if he paid the bail-bondsman, then he might find himself being held liable for the entire hundred thousand, especially since he was Pam's husband.

I told him, "Don't even consider it. Go to court. I think you'll win. If she's still in jail, it's to your advantage."

I started working on formatting my Mary Ellen stories for printing but had little time for it. I had a lot of material and I needed to decide if was going to do a really fat book, omit some stories, or plan for a second book in the future. When Forrest finished with his survival course, he called and we discussed the book project. I had a couple of stories done and he wanted me to put them on a flash drive for him to see. I didn't have a printer. He asked if he could pick me up for dinner along with the flash drive.

To my total astonishment, he took me to meet his family. I said, "Why didn't you warn me?"

He said, "Because I knew you'd try to duck out if I did. It'll be okay. I've told them you've done some writing and I'm helping you publish. For all they know, you're a three hundred pound middle-aged grandmother. They aren't expecting anything."

Again we crossed Current River at Van Buren but we continued on past the turn to Big Spring and turned right onto a county road labeled M. A couple of miles up the road, we turned right again. The house was situated with its back right on the river. Forrest took me through the house and glass doors onto a deck where he was attacked by several boys yelling "Uncle Jay." As I stood in the doorway, the last child, a girl, run up to him and he picked her up and tossed her into the air, catching her on the way down. Her face was looking over his shoulder at me and my heart thudded. *It was Sue Ellen!*

Then immediately I knew it wasn't. She was older than Sue Ellen. As Forrest put her down, I estimated her age at 5. But at 3, she would have looked just like Sue Ellen, eyes and all. It was incredible.

Then a woman moved toward me laughing and said, "They're a mob. I'm Jay's sister, Johanna."

She held out her hand and I shook it, managing to say, "I'm Dria Davis."

"Dria," the woman repeated, "that's unusual. Come and meet the crowd."

She was tall and lanky with dark hair and brown eyes. Both of her parents were the same. They were Jenny and James. James introduced his mother, white-haired and neat looking, as Ruth. Forrest had her eyes.

She took my hand when introduced and said, "I see Jay has found you."

I wanted to say, *What do you mean?* but didn't dare. She looked at me and smiled. I remembered my glimpse of Forrest and I getting married and felt confused. I wondered if she had the Sight. Had she seen it too?

She still had my hand and she turned and said, "Boys!" They all looked up including Forrest. "This is Dria and she's an important person. This tallest one is Jimmy, then Joe, then Jerry, and then Jacob. They all had brown eyes and dark hair. "And this is Mary Ruth," she said, indicating the girl. Only the girl had her grandmother's eyes.

Mary Ruth looked at me and said, "She has funny colored eyes too."

"Yes," I said, "sometimes it's fun and sometimes it's awkward."

She moved over to me and took my other hand and looking up at Forrest said, "Do we get to keep her?"

He grinned and said, "We'll see." But his voice sounded like a yes.

I had a marvelous time. His parents were both teachers. His grandmother said she had taught a few years before she married. Now she quilted and belonged to a garden club.

Joanna's husband, Billy Joe, arrived later. He also was tall but more burly with light brown hair and blue eyes.

Later Forrest's grandmother drew me aside and asked me about my family. I asked if she knew about Forrest rescuing me. She didn't so I told her about my father, about my step-mother hiring the bounty hunters, and about Forrest showing up with Granny and the Marines. "That's Jay," she said, smiling.

"You do have the Sight too, don't you?" she said.

I caught my breath. "Maybe," I said. "Sometimes," I added.

"I normally never talk about it. I never told Jay anything about the Sight. I didn't think he had it. When he graduated from high school, he wanted to marry Ella so he enlisted in the Marines. Then over there in the middle-east war, he found out he did."

She sighed and said, "When his wife was lying over at Springfield in the hospital, I thought we were going to lose him too. But he snapped out of it." She paused and then said, "I need to ask you something."

I suddenly had an odd feeling in the pit of my stomach and then she said, "When you saw Mary Ruth, you turned pale and I saw a picture of you with a child looking like Mary Ruth but younger. You were teaching her to read."

She waited. I didn't know what to say.

Finally she said, "As you get older, you get better at understanding what you're seeing. I suppose that picture could be the future but it felt like now, within the last few days. I think that child already exists and she's Jay's daughter. I know it."

She waited but what could I say? Then she said, "I don't know why you don't want to talk about her but if there's ever a problem, come to me." Later she passed me a slip of paper with a phone number on it.

On the way home, I said, "Your family calls you Jay."

"Yes," he said. "They always have. Forrest was my mother's maiden name. My son was Little Jay." He sounded sad but not wiped out.

"Your sister's children are great," I commented.

"Yes," he said, smiling. "I give their parents a break at times and take them fishing or canoeing or hiking. Mary Ruth is old enough now to want to go too but it's awkward having only one girl along. Will you go with us sometime?"

"Maybe," I said, but I had seen a picture and I knew sometime in the future I would.

When we were on our way home, I called Granny. Forrest said, "You always call when you're on you way home."

"Since the kidnapping, they worry about me."

He looked at me and then said, "It feels more like you need to warn them I'm coming. I bet we find Glen gone again. Is Pam really such an issue with him?"

I didn't know what to say.

Then he said, "It's something about Sue Ellen, isn't it? Is she Down Syndrome or something?"

I managed to nod. Out of honesty, I wanted to add "or something" but didn't.

Forrest said, "My father had a sister who was Down Syndrome. She's dead now but I grew up around her. It was part of what gave me the idea for my Orphan Arthur stories. Tell Glen he doesn't have to hide her from me."

I nodded and asked him when he was planning his next survival training course.

"Soon," he said. "I was surprised at the response for the father-and-son venue. I think I'll have another one soon. Billy Joe wants to come and bring Jimmy so I need to plan it when he can get off work."

So we discussed the survival training courses until we arrived back at the store. Sure enough, Glen and Sue Ellen were gone. Forrest looked at me and grinned.

Granny told him the crew of Amish men were coming tomorrow to begin work on the antique mall booths, including the mezzanine. They thought they could get it done in two days. If they didn't, then the Millers could finish it.

Forrest said he had things to do tomorrow but he would come help the next day.

After he was gone, I told Granny, "Forrest is really beginning to wonder why he never sees Sue Ellen. Today he asked me if she was Down Syndrome or something and I nodded. I should have added 'or something' but he would have asked what. It's starting to get really awkward."

Granny sighed. "I was afraid of that. Forrest and I got to be friends before Glen moved back up here. Glen needs family. In a few years when this is going good, I can sell out and we can move to Alaska or Florida or somewhere but I've lived here all my life. I'm going to talk to Glen about moving back to Poplar Bluff right now, but he thinks I need him, and really I do."

"Is there anyone you can send Sue Ellen to stay with, just for a while?" I asked.

"I can't think of anyone off-hand," she said.

"Maybe we can send her to stay with the Amish. Forrest never goes there."

I was joking but Granny said, "It's a thought. I'll talk to Glen."

The Amish men showed up and they were fast and efficient. They used a lot of non-powered tools but on this project they also used

Granny's power tools. On Tuesday, I made a run for stock and took Sue Ellen. I knew Forrest would notice but what else could we do?

Wednesday was peaceful with John Miller and his son, Samuel, finishing up a few things. The electrician had arrived with a young helper and they got busy.

The next morning was Thursday and I took Sue Ellen out to the garden. We picked produce and then I hoed and weeded. When Sue Ellen got bored, she wandered off to her play house under the pecan tree. She went to the toilet and then washed her hands. I was keeping an eye on her but encouraging her to do things for herself.

Glen came down from his ladder and moved it to the next window. He came over for a drink of water and then sat down at the picnic table. I left the garden and sat down beside him.

"Granny talked to me about taking Sue Ellen back to Poplar Bluff or sending her somewhere until I can move," he said.

"Forrest asked about her and he's really beginning to wonder," I hesitated. "He's a perceptive man, difficult to hide anything from."

"Do you and he have something going?" His voice was even, calm.

"Not really," I said. "I'm cautious about him."

"Sue Ellen loves you," he said. "If I were free, I'd be asking you to marry me." I heard the intensity in his voice.

"Glen," I said. "You're a good man. I respect you. But I'm only 20. I have a lot of time. I love Sue Ellen but any normal woman would. She's a delight.'

"Do you really think the court will give me full custody?" he asked.

"Yes. We'll send Granny to court with you."

Glen smiled. "Granny has a pretty strong opinion about Pam."

"So do a few other people," I commented.

Friday morning early, we saw a school bus pulling in to park in front of the store. I immediately went to call Glen who was painting. When I went into the store, a lady bus driver was saying urgently, "I've gotta have a bathroom."

Granny directed her behind the counter and through the curtain to the downstairs bathroom. "I told those kids to stay on the bus," she yelled as she dived into the facility.

I heard Glen's voice saying, "You can't all come in at once." It was a crowd of high school students. School was out for the summer so I didn't know where they were going but outside at the tail end of the mob, I saw a few adults.

I said, "Your bus driver told you all to stay on the bus."

"I gotta pee," one boy said.

I said, "The toilet is outside around the back of the building."

Glen said, "All of you turn around and go back out the door." He sounded like the voice of authority and most of the kids stopped.

"I wanna coke," one boy said.

"You will be allowed in the store three at a time," Glen announced.

I heard a muttered obscenity and Glen said, "No foul language or you won't be allowed in at all."

One of the adults had managed to push his way inside and Glen said to him, "Students will be admitted to the store only three at a time. The toilet is outside around the building. There is a picnic table around there and a water tap."

The man said, "Okay, everybody, outside." I decided he must be a teacher because they went.

As they filed back out, my eyes checked the Amish display near the door. "Granny," I asked, "are we missing a jar of honey?"

The teacher sent it back in with one of the girls. She said, "The jerk says he was going to buy it so Coach sent me in to see how much."

The students started coming in three at a time. I stood by the door with Sue Ellen and Granny took money. Glen roamed. When three of the biggest boys came in together, I knew one of them was our mutterer. He looked at me with defiance in his eyes and I watched as they tried to huddle over in the hardware. Then I heard an extreme obscenity. Glen barked, "Okay, you three, out!" The boy was taller than him and had his two cohorts but Glen was facing them with no apparent fear.

I said, "This is all being recorded on our surveillance system."

The tallest boy looked around wildly and then started for the door.

The two other boys started to follow him but I heard Granny yelling. I said, "Glen, they need to empty their pockets." They emptied.

I went to the back door and heard Glen talking to the coach.

I shut the wooden back door and locked it. I checked on the sick bus driver and returned to the store. Glen returned to the store and said to me, "Thanks. That was good thinking. I could have handled the ringleader by himself but one of the other boys would definitely have joined him and then the other one would have followed."

"With all this research I've been doing on surveillance systems, it went through my mind that it was too bad we didn't have one in place already and then I thought of saying we did. I'm not normally a liar but I was scared."

Outside the window, we saw the coach marching his students back to the bus. They had come from Ellsinore and were on their way to Van Buren for a one day sports camp. I checked on the bus driver and she said, "They're going to have to get someone else to drive. I've got the runs really bad."

Glen said, "I've got a license to drive a bus but they have to clear it with their people for insurance purposes and they can probably send another driver from Ellsinore."

I went out and told the coach. He said, "Drat, We're going to be late." I told him Glen was a Poplar Bluff school teacher and had a bus license but said it would probably be better if they could get one of their own drivers.

The coach made phone calls and came in and asked Glen to drive them. They had no one else available and it had been cleared. They would even pay.

So Glen left with the bus. I saw the coach had our foul language expert sitting by him.

The lady bus driver was named Janice Jones. She asked if we had anything in the store to stop diarrhea. Granny said, "Yes, but that may not be a good idea. I had a problem once and was taking that stuff and got really sick. Doctor told me why people get the runs is because there's something their body needs to get rid of. He said if you put a stop to it, you can get even sicker. He said taking one dose so you could get to a doctor was okay but no more than that. He said drink a lot of water and if it lasted more than a few hours, to drink a rehydration drink."

Then Granny said, "This sort of thing usually lets up in little while. If it really doesn't quit, then we'll try a dose of that stuff so you can get home."

Sue Ellen wanted to show off her reading skills and Janice obliged, between bathroom breaks. "Is she really reading?" she asked.

"I'm not sure yet," I said. "We're just getting started and she's a good memorizer."

I asked about opportunities in Ellsinore for work as a pre-school teacher. She said, "We have a Head Start program. Can you substitute teach? They always need subs and I heard they're suddenly looking for a high school history teacher. Mrs. Carter has taught for years but she had a heart attack about a week ago."

Granny said, "My grandson has been teaching history and PE at the high school in Poplar Bluff."

Our sick bus driver found the idea of an antique store and flea market interesting. She said, "It'd be nice if it's not one of those really horrid places full of dirty junk."

Granny said, "The Amish are planning to have a booth and I can't see Amish women putting up with anything like that."

Gloria's mother was coming once a month to help Granny dust the whole store and clean anything which looked dirty. They even moved the meat case, refrigerator case, and freezer on a rotating schedule and cleaned underneath them. Granny left the door open between the living quarters and the store at night and Lady often spent the night in the store. Granny said, "I leave my bedroom door open so she can wake me up if she wants out."

Glen returned from his trip to Van Buren and told us the coach had also told him about the teaching job and even said he would mention him to the superintendent. Glen said, "If it weren't for the problem about Sue Ellen, I would jump on it." He sighed. "Maybe he'd not think about her being his."

Granny and I both knew who *he* was. I said, "He would. He's talked about Pam and his son had those same eyes."

"He talked about Pam!" Glen was surprised.

"He knew you were dodging him and I said maybe it was because of Pam." I paused, not sure how much I should say. "He said he was sorry it ever happened."

Glen looked glum. "Surely he wouldn't want Sue Ellen. If I just went and talked to him, do you think he'd stay out if it?"

I had entertained the same question. I reluctantly said, "I don't know for sure but he was very fond of his son and he's quite involved with his sister's kids."

Glen shook his head.

I said, "Yes, it would be much easier if he was a terrible man but he isn't."

Granny said, "We need to do some serious praying."

Chapter 12: The Fight

The next morning, even though it was Saturday, Glen got a call from the Ellsinore Superintendent. He wanted to interview him on Monday. Glen explained he had already signed a contract with Poplar Bluff but the man said, "I can talk to them."

I was outside with Sue Ellen. I went through the *Green Eggs and Ham* book with her again, having her point to each word as she said it. Then we practiced writing in the dirt. She had her name down pat and wanted to learn *Daddy*. She seemed to get it quickly and then went to her playhouse under the pecan tree.

I was sitting at the picnic table in the shade of an oak tree sketching Sue Ellen. I had done at least two dozen sketches of Sue Ellen. Now I was catching her at play.

Then I saw her stand up and look intently at something hidden from my sight by the pump house. She said, "Who awe you?"

A man stepped out from behind the small building and said, "I'm a friend of Dria's. Who are you?"

"Ssue Ellen," she said, buzzing her s sound. "Can you wead?" she asked.

"Yes," he answered.

I was frozen, not even breathing. Sue Ellen said, "Come ssit and I'll wead *Gween Eggss and Ham*."

Then Forrest said, "Do you like green eggs and ham?"

Sue Ellen giggled and started for the picnic table where I sat and where she had left her book. "Here'ss my book. I can wead it for you."

"Really," he said. "Please read it for me."

I watched as she went through the book, pointing to each word.

When she finished, Forrest said, "You're a smart little girl."

"I'm a good little giwl," she informed him. "I behave nice and I say my pwayers."

"Do you?" he said. "That's good."

Sue Ellen got up and said, "I'm playing housth," and went back to the pecan tree.

Forrest glanced at my sketchbook and reached over and picked it up. He looked at what I had been doing and then turned it back to the beginning and studied it page by page without saying a word.

I simply sat, silent. I didn't know what to say.

When he came back to where I was working today, he laid the book down and looked at me. "Pam called me," he said. "I wouldn't have answered if I had known it was her but she was calling from the jail over in Branson." He looked back at Sue Ellen playing contently with her stick people. "She wants money so she told me about Sue Ellen. I thought she was lying but I had to come see."

He stood up, ran his hand through his hair, and said, "I have to talk to Glen." He strode off, going through the back door where he had often gone before.

I told Sue Ellen it was time to quit and go eat lunch. I heard raised voices and so did Sue Ellen. We were both looking at the back door when Forrest came through it again. Glen burst through behind him shouting, "You can't have her." But Forrest was headed our way.

I scooped up Sue Ellen, not sure what to do but Glen suddenly launched himself onto Forrest's back and they both went down on the ground, rolling and wrestling and yelling. Sue Ellen started crying.

I moved over near them yelling, "Stop! Stop!"

Then somehow Forrest got Glen down on his stomach with his arm twisted up behind his back. I remembered Forrest was an ex-Marine with combat experience. He knew how to fight.

Sue Ellen was screaming. I yelled, "Stop it! Stop it! You two are scaring Sue Ellen."

Forrest looked up at the distraught child and slowly released Glen and stood up. Glen got up and Sue Ellen reached out to him, crying, "Daddy. Daddy."

I moved to hand her to him and she clung to him like a stick-tight seed.

Forrest said quietly, intently, "I'm getting a lawyer," and stomped away.

I got my phone and found the slip of paper with the phone number Forrest's grandmother had given me. I said, "This is Dria. Forrest needs you. Can you come?"

"The child?" she asked.

"Yes," I said. "He just found out about her."

I got in my car and drove to Forrest's house. No one responded to the gate. I got out and walked. I rang the doorbell but no one came. His jeep was parked near the front door so I went in. I climbed the stairs and heard his voice coming from his study.

When I went in, he stopped talking on the phone and said to me, "Get out!"

I looked at him and saw past the anger to the hurt and the instant love for a child he knew was his. He was a fierce man and could be dangerous but I was not afraid. I walked over and sat down in the chair I had used before.

He said into the phone, "I'll be in to see you."

He looked at me and said, "Get out of my house! You helped hide her! You knew and you were in on it! Get out!"

I said calmly, "There is something you need to know."

He said, "What I needed to know was that I'm her father! She's mine!"

I said, "If Glen had not married her mother, Sue Ellen would not be alive."

"What!" he said.

I said, trying to keep my voice calm. "Pam wanted Glen to pay for an abortion but just like you, he wouldn't. He had some money and he used it to get her to marry him. Pam never took care of Sue Ellen. Glen did. He told me that she was 2 before he realized she wasn't his. He said by that time, he didn't care who Pam had been sleeping with, Sue Ellen was his daughter. He loves her. He didn't know who her biological father was until you came to help with clean-up after the vandalism. If it wasn't for Glen, Pam would have found a way to get an abortion."

Forrest ran his fingers through his hair. "Damnation!" he said. "I'd like to throttle that woman."

"You'd have to take a number and stand in line."

He didn't laugh but he did calm down.

"Glen loves Sue Ellen," I said. "He wants what's best for her and I think you do too."

"You lied to me," he said.

"A little," I agreed. "It bothered me not to add 'or something' but if I had, you would have demanded to know what."

"What else have you lied to me about?"

"Only about Sue Ellen," I said. "Well, to be perfectly honest, I would not have gone to dinner with you if I hadn't been helping hide Sue Ellen."

He shook his head. "So you prefer Glen."

"I don't prefer anyone!" I said. "I haven't known either one of you long enough to get serious."

"I'm going to my lawyer," he said.

I said, "Forrest, you saw how Sue Ellen wanted Glen. Pam has never been a mother to her. All of her security has been Glen. He may not be her biological father but he's her psychological father. She loves him. She needs him. I know you want her and if Glen was not a good parent, I'd tell you to take her away in a minute, but he is a good parent and she's attached to him. You'll hurt her by taking her away."

He looked at me and run his hand through his hair again. "Hell and damnation!" he said.

If the situation had not been so serious, I would have smiled. After some of the language I had heard at collage, his curses sounded quaint.

"What am I going to do?" he muttered, looking out the window, and I knew he was not asking me but talking to himself.

"I called your grandmother," I said. "She's on her way."

His head came back around and his eyes fastened on to mine. "You called my grandmother? Why?"

"The other day, at your parent's house, she saw Sue Ellen. She told me. She knew it was not a vision of the future or the past, but now. She saw me setting with Sue Ellen teaching her to read. She gave me her phone number and told me to call her if I thought she was needed."

"The Sight," Forrest said and he looked haunted. "It's a curse."

I nodded. "Sometimes. And sometimes it's a blessing."

"What can Grandma do?"

"Old people have more life experience. They often can give good advice. Maybe her and Granny can think of something."

"Granny will take Glen's side."

"Forrest, I'm taking sides – Sue Ellen's. If you went back to the store right now, the child would look at you and cry. You were fighting with her daddy. Glen has always been there for her. She loves him. Think! Think what's best for Sue Ellen."

He looked at me for a full minute in silence and then turned his head and looked out the windows again. I waited, silent. What else was there to say?

Then I realized that tears were rolling down Forrest's face. With no thought, I stood and moved over and put my hand on his shoulder. He turned and looked up at me, the face of tragedy. "It's my fault," he said. "I let her seduce me and I knew it was wrong. Then when she said she was pregnant, I knew what a liar she was so I didn't even check. I don't deserve Sue Ellen, do I?"

He began sobbing and I gathered him into my arms. As I held him, I prayed, for him, for Sue Ellen, for all of us. He sobbed for at least two minutes on my shoulder with his arms around my waist. I held him and let him cry. Then he pulled himself together, took a deep breath, and pulled away. I turned loose of him and then, without thinking, as though he was Sue Ellen, I leaned over and placed a small kiss on his forehead.

I stepped back and then heard a voice coming up the stairs. "Jay, are you up there?" It was Forrest's grandmother.

She came through the door, stopped and looked from Forrest to me and back to him. She came in and putting her purse on Forrest's desk, she sat down in the chair where I had sat before. "Tell me all about it," she said.

Forrest sighed and looked at me. I said, "I'll go." He didn't stop me.

Back at the store, I found Glen packing Sue Ellen's things. He was planning to take her and run. I said, "I don't think you need to go."

He looked at me with sorrow in his eyes and I said, "I talked to Forrest. I got him to listen."

"Why would he listen to you?" he asked.

"He had already told me about his relationship with Pam. He felt guilty about it. She had tried to get him to pay for an abortion but like you, he wouldn't. He also knew she was a liar. He told her he'd go to the doctor with her and if she was pregnant, he'd pay her medical bills but he would keep the baby. She didn't. Instead she married you so he assumed if she was really pregnant, it was yours."

"He was willing to keep a baby but he wasn't willing to marry her?"

"At the time this happened, his wife was lying in a coma. Granny knew him already then. She says he was drinking."

"Pam!" Glen said, with his voice reflecting bitterness, "I'd like to send her straight to hell!"

I said, "You and me and Granny and Forrest and his grandmother too when he gets through telling her all about it."

"His grandmother!" Glen exclaimed. "How did she get involved with this?"

"He's close to her and . . . and she sees things. Forrest was actually crying over the situation. She'll help him sort himself out."

"Crying?" Glen's voice projected his disbelief.

"He feels guilty," I said.

Glen looked at me sharply and then turned away. "I know the feeling," he said.

I said, "I don't think you should run, at least not yet. I think we can work something out. It's not like Forrest has got a wife to help care for a child."

"Neither do I," Glen said.

"No, but you have Granny and Sue Ellen is settled here with you. I told Forrest that psychologically you're her father. You have always been there for her; you have always taken care of her. She knows you. She's happy here."

"Dria," Glen said, looking me full in the eyes, "marry me. When I'm free, marry me."

I shook my head. "Let's deal with the getting free part first. You shouldn't remarry just to provide a mother for Sue Ellen. Give it some time."

Glen looked unhappy. "Forrest has got money. He'll get lawyers and take her away."

"Glen," I said, "Forrest actually cares about Sue Ellen. I don't think he would do anything to hurt her and separating her from you right now would hurt her."

He looked indecisive.

I said, "Let's see what happens."

All the rest of the day, I expected to hear something from Forrest. Granny and I convinced Glen to take Sue Ellen to Poplar Bluff to play at a park or McDonald's. We'd call him when we heard from Forrest.

But Forrest never called or came or anything.

We finally called Glen and he brought a sleeping Sue Ellen home and we put her to bed. He said, "It's the weekend. He can't get a lawyer on a weekend."

Glen didn't know lawyers. I said, "When I went out to his place, he was on the phone and I think he was talking to his lawyer."

Glen come out with a crude word I had never heard him use before. Then he said, "Sorry. This has got me so upset, I don't know what I'm doing."

Granny said, "Nobody's coming in the middle of the night. Get some sleep and we'll see what it looks like tomorrow morning."

That night I spent a long time in prayer. I am deeply attached to Forrest. I don't know when it happened or how it happened, but it had happened. I knew it. Am I in love with him? I'm not sure but I think maybe it's what has happened.

I don't know what to do. I laid it all out before God and pleaded for help.

Chapter 13: The Lawyer

The next day was Sunday and I took Sue Ellen and went to visit Cousin Marie. I told Glen, "You stay here where Forrest can find you. Besides, you need to pull your paperwork together for your interview tomorrow."

At Cousin Marie's I asked for help and Maggie said her daughter and her teenage granddaughter might be willing to keep Sue Ellen for a few days. I met them and phoned Glen and we arranged it. I told them, "I don't expect you to lie to anyone so if someone official shows up, just call us and let us know."

Glen packed some things for Sue Ellen including her books and some favorite toys and came to meet Maggie's daughter and granddaughter. He talked to Sue Ellen. I warned him to be careful about showing he was upset. He said, "I know. It amazes me sometimes what she picks up on. I didn't know small children could be so sensitive."

I thought, *And some much more than others. She's her father's daughter.*

Glen told Sue Ellen he had work to do tomorrow and for a few days. He said it was like the daycare where she used to go while he worked and he would be back to get her when it was time. She looked at him and I saw Forrest in her look. "I don't want you to go to wowk."

He smiled at her. "I know. I don't want to but I have to go."

She nodded and I thought how she'd learned already that life isn't always what you want it to be.

Monday morning Glen went for his interview. He said, "I can't even think about anything but this mess with Sue Ellen." But he took his paperwork and went.

He came back saying the superintendent, the high school principal, the coach, and the chairperson of the school board had all been there. He said, "I think somehow they had already made up their minds they wanted me but they said it has to go to the school board. They meet tomorrow evening. That's why they wanted to interview me today."

Monday afternoon a lawyer showed up to talk to Glen. We assumed it was about Sue Ellen but the man said, "I've got papers here for your divorce." He said Pam was willing to give him an uncontested divorce. All Glen had to do was sign papers and appear in court.

Glen said, "What about Sue Ellen?"

The lawyer said, "I also have papers concerning the child. I have here an affidavit signed by your wife stating that the biological father of the child is a man named James Forrest Hunter. She has signed papers giving up all of her parental rights to Mr. Hunter." I saw the look of dismay on Glen's face and I knew the lawyer saw it too but he went on without regarding it. "Mr. Hunter has signed papers saying that at this time, he is willing to leave the child in your custody but reserves the right to call for a custody hearing if he sees need for it in the future. If you are willing to agree to this, we can deal with it in the same court hearing."

"It's my name on Sue Ellen's birth certificate!" Glen said fiercely. Glen was rubbing his left elbow which I knew he did when he was upset. Granny said he'd broken it once years ago playing basketball.

"Yes," the lawyer agreed. "Mr. Hunter said he knew you loved the child and you seemed to be doing a good job of parenting her."

Glen exhaled audibly. He looked off, thinking, and then after a silent minute of rubbing his elbow, looked back at the lawyer and said, "What does he mean by reserving the right to call for a custody hearing the future?"

"Right now, Mr. Hunter is doing some traveling. He said later, he would talk to you. He says the child is settled here with you and he doesn't want to upset her life." The lawyer paused and then went on, "He said it was not popular now-a-days to talk about sin but he said it was his sin which led to this situation and he needed to take responsibility for it. He instructed me to tell you if the child needed anything you could not provide, to contact me."

"But if he has access to her, he will try to entice her away. He has money. He can buy her things I can't afford." Glen's tone was belligerent.

The lawyer looked at Glen without flinching. He said, "Mr. Hunter said to tell you he was aware that nothing is worse for a child than two parents working against each other. He said to tell you he doesn't want that for his daughter."

Glen was still glaring and I spoke up. "Glen, I know Forrest better than you do. If he said that, he meant it. Saturday when I went out to talk to him, I told him to think about what was best for Sue Ellen. I think you can trust him to do that."

"Trust him?" Glen's voice was hard. "He slept with Pam and then dumped her! Why should I trust him?"

"You know it wasn't exactly like that. Pam just decided she could get more out of you. Forrest can be pretty scary when he's mad."

Glen said with a wry face, "That's true." He was still rubbing his elbow and it occurred to me his arm probably still hurt from his fight with Forrest. It had been his left arm twisted behind his back.

In the end, Glen signed the papers. I read them all through, telling the lawyer my father had been a lawyer and I had worked some in his office.

After he packed up all the papers, he said to me, "Miss Davis, can I have a private word with you?"

With raised eyebrows, I agreed and took him out to the picnic table under the oak tree in the back yard.

He settled and waited for me to settle before starting. "Mr. Hunter asked me to make a request of you. He says you have met his family. He would like for Sue Ellen to get to know them." He paused and then went on. "He says his grandmother was an orphan and you all might could agree on a story of a distant relationship. I'm not sure why he thinks that's necessary but it's what he said."

I smiled. "You haven't seen Sue Ellen," I said. "She has Forrest's eyes. They're his grandmother's eyes and his sister's daughter has them as well. I'm sure half the neighbors around here have already figured out he's her father. Glen knew the first time he got a good look at Forrest. That's why we were all trying to keep Forrest from seeing the child. We knew he'd know instantly. So will his family."

The man shook his head. "I've been Mr. Hunter's lawyer for years. He's a strange man in some ways but if he says something, he'll stick to it. He said if you refused his request, he would not insist, but he thought you would do it."

I smiled. "Every child needs family and more grandparents are helpful. An aunt and uncle and cousins are nice too. I'll see what I can work out."

The man was started to rise and I asked, "What about Forrest? Is he okay?"

The man settled again, looking at me intently. "He's fine. He said he was going to travel for a while."

I looked at him, thinking over the picture I had just seen. I sighed. "He's searching for something," I said.

"He didn't tell me why he was traveling." He gathered up his things and left.

When he was gone, I called and Glen and I went after Sue Ellen. She said she'd had fun and liked that daycare. I told her she could come here again sometime.

Tuesday night, Glen got a phone call. He had the job at Ellsinore providing Poplar Bluff would release him from his contract without prejudice. Then the superintendent told Glen he was sure they would. He said, "I had another applicant I think they'll hire in your place."

Glen found out later it was the bus trip to Van Buren which got him the job. When they started out, someone had hit Glen with a paper wad. He pulled the bus over and announced calmly he didn't have to drive their bus and if they wanted to get to Van Buren, no more paper wads. There was. He stopped again and said, "Sorry, guys. You want to get to Van Buren, you'll have to get another driver." He had gotten off the bus, crossed the road, and started walking with his thumb out. The coach said other students pointed out the culprit and then they talked Glen into coming back. The coach had told the superintendent, "We always have trouble on the bus going to and from sports events and he got them over a barrel. He can handle discipline and that's two-thirds of teaching."

The electrician finished his work on Wednesday and so did the plumber. The water came on first and there were leaks which is what the plumber had expected. The water went on and off so many times, I finally stationed myself at the shut off valve and we arranged a signaling system. But by early evening, the electricity and the water were both working.

The men took their checks, shook hands with us, and the plumber said, "It's a grand old building and well arranged. With the proper care, it'll be here another hundred years. I'll be back in the fall to see to the boiler and heating system. Bound to be a few leaks but nothing we can't handle."

Granny had purchased a surveillance system, a computer, and a bookkeeping system for the antique mall. A man had been working on installation of the security cameras on Wednesday and would be back on Thursday morning to finish and make sure we knew how to use it. When he started showing us, he kept focusing on me and it occurred to me he was thinking Granny was too old for a computer. I told him, "It's Granny you need to make sure knows how to do this. She's the owner. I'm just a temporary employee."

The young man was surprised at how quickly Granny was getting it. I said to him, "She's kept books the old-fashioned way for years. She loves her new bookkeeping program for the general store. It saves a lot of time and she's delighted with it's accuracy. If you need an advocate for computers, recruit Granny."

The surveillance installer warned us the worst problem businesses had with thievery was often their own employees. When I had been doing my research, I had been warned several times to keep an eye on our vendors. It was not uncommon for some to steal from other vendors as they carried boxes in and out while stocking their own booths.

Friday the vendors started moving in and it was a circus. One woman looked at the radiator in her booth space and said, "What's this? I want it out of here!" Granny told her it was her winter heat and the woman said, "What! I want electric heat."

Granny said, "If you want modern style heat, you'll have to rent a space in a modern building. This is an antique building with antique heating. It works good and it's economical to run so we're keeping it. When we rented this space, we explained you had to keep everything off it in winter. The plumber said at least a foot in all directions and two feet over it. Even then, he said nothing that will melt." On the outside wall, the radiators were located under the windows.

Granny offered the woman a booth on the inside of the aisle or on the mezzanine but the woman's pardner had rented the space. She said, "I thought the radiator was cute, real antiquey, and I wanted a window for displaying stained glass." Gloria had helped Glen give the radiators a new coat of some kind of paint designed for heat. I hadn't known there was such a thing.

I also learned one function of the ceiling fans was to circulate air so temperatures in the large room stayed even.

The Amish had a double booth at the beginning of the first row on the outside wall. They filled it with furniture, small wooden items, quilts, bonnets, and a few Amish dresses. Granny had decided no clothes but she said a few pieces like costumes, wedding dresses, and vintage clothing were allowed.

More than half the booths were already rented. Only one arriving vendor looked like a problem. He hauled in crates of junk which he stacked in the booth. When asked if he planned to bring shelves for display, he said, "No need. They can just dig through the boxes and find what they want."

Granny said, "You were told you had to keep your booth clean, neat, and tidy. This doesn't qualify. I think you need to just load back up right now and find another place." He grumbled and muttered but took his junk and left. Someone told us he normally sold stuff at open air markets like the one in Poplar Bluff on Friday mornings.

We were opening on Monday for business but were holding a Grand Opening event on the following Saturday. The Amish men had built Granny a new, larger sign, and Glen had painted it. It said, "Davis General Store, Bed and Breakfast, Antique Mall" and at the bottom in much smaller letters, it said, "Antiques, Handcrafts, Collectibles, Etc." Glen had wanted to put "junk" but Granny was afraid some vendors would take it literally. However, she had found a sign which said "We Buy Junk and Sell Antiques" and had hung it near the cash register.

The old cash register had been moved to the antique store and Glen had installed a new computer operated one in the general store which kept the books and produced receipts for the customers.

Business was up at the general store and wholesalers who delivered to stores in Van Buren suddenly wanted Granny's business again. She accepted some but rejected others, not only on grounds of cost but also quality. She said going after our own produce was better and besides, with the word out, she was getting more local stuff.

Glen had made a banner saying "Grand Opening Saturday" and hung it out on the new sign. Saturday was a fine day so we carried the picnic table around to the front and sold twenty-five cent hot dogs and twenty-five cent canned sodas. Gloria and her mother were helping and so were some of the Amish.

Samuel Miller had come and he soon was giving buggy rides. That had not been planned but someone asked and offered to pay so Samuel took them down to the church and back. He returned to find more customers waiting.

Granny watched the surveillance and caught a thief. Do thieves not take gray-haired grandmothers seriously? Granny said, "This is more fun than watching TV."

By mid-afternoon we had booked all six of our rooms for the night. Gloria and Sofie were developing a friendship. The veterinarian in Van Buren had said no to Gloria. He had two boys in training already. The Amish had horses and other animals. Sofie invited Gloria out to see their farm and now her mother said she was out there more than she was home. I noticed Gloria had not only gotten contacts, she was no longer slumping. Samuel Miller was taller than her and I wondered if he had anything to do with her spending so much time out there.

Saturday evening, we did not close until dark. Our guests for the night were still running around and we realized we had not thought about needing to lock the door at the top of the stairs going from the guest rooms into the antique store. Not only did we not want guests to have access to the store at night but also we did not want patrons in the store sneaking into the guest rooms during the day. The rooms all had locks but the keys were just skeleton keys and it was not difficult to buy master keys. So Granny produced a lot of keys and Glen oiled the lock in the door and tried keys until he found one which worked.

Glen and Granny and I did not get to bed until midnight and I woke up the next morning to find Sue Ellen had gotten up, dressed herself, and was busy with her Legos.

We did breakfast for the guests. We had taken orders and times the night before. We had set the old hotel lounge up as a combination lounge and dining room. I sent Granny, Glen, and Sue Ellen to church while I dealt with the late risers. We had a large sign for the antique store saying "Closed Sundays" and the general store had its "Closed: For Urgent Needs, Ring Bell" sign. Some of our guests were still here and they found it quaint. I told them normally on Sunday mornings we put out a "Closed for Church" sign.

One couple had asked for directions and gone to church. They came back and asked to stay another night. They went off to Van Buren and the natural beauty of the Ozark National Scenic Riverways.

Sunday afternoon several cars pulled in and left. No one rang the bell. Granny laughed and said she wasn't surprised because all her usual Sunday customers were here yesterday. She said, "For a long time now, I've thought they're just too lazy to plan ahead and they know I'm here."

Glen suggested he make two small signs, one saying "Open" and one saying "Closed" and attach two hooks to the bottom of our big sign near the highway. We could then hang them out where everyone would see them. He said it would lessen frustration for tourists who expected everything to be open on Sunday.

Gloria's mother told us Forrest had called her and had her meet his sister and a workman who came over to close up his house. He asked her if she would go over once a week and check everything.

I felt sad. Forrest clearly planned to be gone for some time. I considered what he could be looking for but it wasn't clear. Forrest somehow had left a hole in my life. As little as I had seen of him, how could he have left such an empty place?

I must be in love with him. I could think of no other explanation. Christians are not suppose to marry non-Christians. I thought somewhere deep down, Forrest believed, but I also wondered if I was engaging in wishful thinking.

I found myself praying for him and for me, asking God to take total control of my heart.

Chapter 14: To Court

The business developed into a pretty steady stream of people with recognizable peaks at lunch time, when people were getting home from work, on Friday afternoons, and on Saturdays starting about mid-morning. The general store had always done a good trade during lunch time in sandwiches but now it doubled. The bed and breakfast people were up and down but Friday night was often full. Our most frequent guests were people who stopped for the antique store and decided to stay. We did breakfast from 7 to 9 so people were out of the way by 10 and by 9:30 on Sunday mornings. We continued to close on Sundays although many people had told us we should open on Sunday afternoons but the Amish were totally against it and really, so was Granny. She said, "I don't mind obliging when someone needs baby formula or milk but just to do business on the Sabbath like it was any other day of the week doesn't seem right."

We had clear "No Smoking" signs everywhere and when people asked about a room, we told them no smoking was allowed in the rooms or anywhere in the building. They could smoke on the porches, either front or back, but no where inside. The first Friday night, we had a violator and didn't know it until we cleaned rooms Saturday. After that, we posted a notice saying there would be a fifty dollar cleaning fee for smoking inside and we checked rooms before people left.

Gloria's mother started working regularly on Fridays and Granny worked out an arrangement with the Amish where the women worked in exchange for their booth rent. They made a stand-up sign saying "Amish Buggy Rides" and on Saturdays, Sofie often put it out and made some money. Samuel was needed at home. Sofie would only take couples and families. If it was a man, or even an odd looking couple, she came in and worked in Glen's place while he did it. He had a pair of overalls he started wearing on Saturdays if they were doing buggy rides. It was amazing how many people wanted to ride in an Amish buggy.

Glen's court date came up and he was required to bring Sue Ellen so Granny and I went too. He had filed for the divorce in Carter County but had agreed to a change of venue to Taney County where Branson was located because of Pam being in jail there.

Another thing which had come up was Pam's car, a Mustang, on which Glen was making payments and carrying insurance. When he learned Pam was in jail, he wanted to pick up her car but discovered Ray had wrecked it and the insurance company was still stalling on paying out. The wrecked car was now no where to be found. It was a problem and Glen filed a police report, stopped making payments, and refused to continue insurance payments on it. It was insured for theft but the insurance company did not want to pay as they thought Ray and his cohorts had stripped it out and sold the parts or maybe the whole car.

As we entered the courtroom, I saw Joanna first and then Mary Ruth. Grandma Ruth was there too and they were setting on one side of the small courtroom while the judge was dealing with another case. I had stopped short when I saw them but Granny and Glen with Sue Ellen went on and moved into the row of seats behind them. They were looking on the other side of the isle where Pam was sitting with the lawyer. I sat down and leaned across Sue Ellen to whisper as softly as possible to Glen, "Forrest's family," and pointed.

I saw Glen about to get up and I put my hand on his arm. "It'll be okay," I whispered.

"Why are they here?" he asked.

"Forrest isn't," I whispered back.

Then Mary Ruth looked around and like any 5-year-old seeing another child in a room of only adults, she twisted in her seat and got up on her knees for a good look.

Glen stared at her in total shock. Then Joanna turned and saw us, then Grandma Ruth. Joanna said to me, "I see you all made it. I think you're up next."

I whispered, "Glen, this is Forrest's sister, Joanna, their grandmother, Ruth, and her daughter, Mary Ruth." Then I said, "This is Glen Davis, his grandmother, Susan Davis, and this is Sue Ellen."

Sue Ellen said, "Can we play?"

"Not now," I said, "but maybe later."

After minute of silence, Glen whispered, "I can't believe it."

I said, "I know. The first time I saw her, I thought it was Sue Ellen."

"They'll take Sue Ellen away," he said. "This was just a trap to get her here."

"No," I said. "Forrest will keep to his word."

The next case was the dissolution of the marriage of Pamela Jean and Glen Herbert Davis and the custody of a child known as Sue Ellen Davis. The judge said, "I have been through the papers concerning this matter and failed to find anything proving paternity."

The lawyer sitting with Pam stood and said, "Your Honor, none of the parties involved in this matter are disputing the paternity of the child."

"Why not?" the judge asked.

The lawyer had everyone but me up to the bench. Evidently they had a good photo of Forrest. The judge looked and said, "Okay. Let the records show that the child in question has inherited an unusual pair of eyes from her biological father which are clearly a characteristic of his family."

The judge then talked to Glen alone up at his bench. He then talked to Pam. Then to Glen again. The lawyer was next and then he wanted Grandma Ruth. Last was Granny Davis. We could not hear what was being said but the court recorder was recording it all and I knew it would go into the court records and I could read it all later if I wished.

As everyone moved around, I watched Pam. I had not seen her

before and more significantly, although Granny had lots of family pictures on display, none of them included Pam. She was taller than average but skinny, maybe anorexic, but what caught my attention was she resembled the photo I had seen on Forrest's desk of his wife, Ella. Maybe that partly explained why Forrest had gotten involved with her.

The judge then announced, "In looking into this marriage, I see grounds for granting an annulment but at the request of Glen Herbert Davis, I am declaring a dissolution of marriage, commonly known as a divorce."

The judge then picked up another set of papers and announced, "Concerning the child known as Sue Ellen Davis, custody is being granted to Glen Herbert Davis and his grandmother, Susan Willamina Davis. The mother of the child, Pamela Jean Davis, has signed papers giving her parental rights to the biological father of the child, James Forrest Hunter. Mr. Hunter is in turn granting custody of the child to the afore mentioned parties. I have stipulated however, if Mr. Hunter has reason in the future to question the suitability of the arrangement, it may be brought back into court."

As we left the courtroom, all of us quiet, still absorbing the rulings. The lawyer quickly took Pam away and neither looked back. Pam had not spoken to Sue Ellen, nor really even looked at her. And Sue Ellen had given no sign of wanting to greet her mother.

After a minute of silence, Forrest's Grandmother said to Granny, "I was thinking the two of us should have a small chat."

Glen picked up Sue Ellen and said, "I'll be down at the car."

The two grandmothers moved off in the other direction and I found myself standing with Joanna and Mary Ruth. I said, "Is Forrest doing okay?"

Joanna smiled and said, "Grandma said you would ask. He's doing some traveling."

"That's all you're going to say, isn't it?"

She sighed, "Yes." Then when I remained silent, she said, "Jay has always been a rather intense person. I think he needs time to sort himself out."

I nodded. "The lawyer told me Forrest wanted Sue Ellen to get to know all of you. He said he wouldn't insist but was requesting. Is that what your Grandmother wanted to talk to Granny about?"

"Maybe. Jay has always talked to Grandma more than to the rest of us."

The two old ladies returned and Forrest's grandmother said, "Mrs. Davis and I have been talking. Everyone knows I was adopted by the Chilton family when I was a baby. Sue Willa and I have discussed our families and we think we're related." She smiled and said, "She thinks maybe my mother was a cousin of her mother's. The family left during the Depression to go to California and were never heard from again."

Joanna smiled and said, "That's possible and it would explain why Sue Ellen has those eyes." The two old ladies looked mischievous.

Joanna said, "While we're here in Branson, we promised Mary Ruth we'd ride the Ducks. Maybe all of us could go together."

Granny and I talked Glen into it. I told him, "With Granny and Grandma Ruth telling everyone they think they're related, no one will ask awkward questions. When Forrest took me over to meet his family, I liked them."

"You don't think Forrest's sister will try to get Sue Ellen?"

I told Glen, "Besides Mary Ruth, Joanna has four boys. I think she has her hands full."

"Four boys!" Glen exclaimed and looked assessingly at Joanna.

We rode the ducks which turned out to be a lot more fun than I expected. However, the traffic in Branson is like Los Angeles in rush hour. When we left, Joanna suggested we follow her and she took some side streets and eventually got us back on Highway 65 North. We stopped at Lambert's Cafe for lunch and I soon saw why it was so popular. Granny said, "I can make rolls like this but it takes a lot of time."

"I want to learn," I said.

Then as we approached Van Buren, we stopped at Forrest's parent's house on the river. Joanna had called and we found hamburgers and hot dogs on the grill with four boys waiting to meet their small cousin. The trip had taken three hours and Sue Ellen had slept in the car. She was ready to play.

The boys accepted the cousin story without question and Forrest's parents had been prepared for it and made all the appropriate remarks. The boys had nice manners and shook hands when introduced. Joe, the second boy, asked, "Can we call you Uncle Glen?" Later I heard him asking Glen, "Do you go canoeing like Uncle Jay? He was going to take us but he's gone off somewhere and won't be back for a while."

"Where has he gone?" Glen asked.

"We don't know," Jerry told him. "He was a Marine. We think he might be on a secret mission."

Jimmy said, "We used to have a cousin called Little Jay. Uncle Jay was his father. Little Jay and his mother got killed and maybe Uncle Jay has gone looking for their killer."

Glen asked, "Didn't they put their killer in prison?"

Jimmy said, "They told Uncle Jay someone killed him but maybe Uncle Jay found out he really got away and now he's gone to get him."

Joanna said, "My boys have wild imaginations. I think they got it from their Uncle Jay. He's always telling them stories on camping trips about Bigfoot and the Ozark Howler."

Jimmy said, "And he wrote some books for Little Jay about an orphan named Arthur. They have kings and queens and knights and witches and dragons and all that. I'll show you," he said.

He went into the house and returned with two of the Orphan Arthur books. These were dogeared and slightly grubby from being handled by little boys. Glen looked at them and said, "Your Uncle Jay wrote these?"

"Sure," Jimmy told him. "And he wrote some books on survival stuff too." I saw the bewildered look on Glen's face.

Then Sue Ellen said, "Let me ssee." She examined one of the books solemnly and pointing to the title said, "The Gween … "

I said, "Dragon," automatically coaching her. Her recognition of a word from another book confirmed she really was learning to read.

"Dwagon," she repeated. "Can I wead it?"

"It's a really big book and we don't have time for it now. Did you bring your book you have been reading?"

She pulled it out of her toy tote and said to Jimmy. "I can wead."

Jimmy let her read to him and was clearly impressed. He said, "She's not even big enough to talk plain and she can read!"

I sat with Forrest's grandmother for a while. I told her, "The first time I went out to Forrest's place, I recognized those illustrations. I had read the series through at least six times."

His grandmother sighed. "He's a complicated man. He confuses people."

As she said it, I had a picture. Forrest was talking to an old man, tall like him, and with the same eyes. I said, "I know you were adopted. Do you know anything about your family at all?"

She looked at me keenly and said, "You've had a Sight."

"I saw Forrest talking to an old man with the same eyes."

She looked away while she thought and then said, "You and me and the gatepost?"

Granny had introduced me to the expression. It meant whatever was said was to go no further. I agreed, "You and me and the gatepost."

"I was found as a newborn baby in a church out in the country from Van Buren. Everyone knows the story and know the Chilton's adopted me. The part they don't know is my mother's body was also found in the church. She had been laid out proper and wrapped in a blanket with a note. The note said she had said it was no use to call a doctor and had said to leave the baby there with her body and some good people would adopt her. They buried my mother in the cemetery by the church. Later they put a small stone just saying 'Mother.'

"Then years later, when I was 13, one day I came out of school and a man was waiting to talk to me."

She paused and I just waited. Finally she said, "He was my father. He told me what happened. He said because of the Depression, there was no work and his family lost their farm. They were evicted from their house and they were camped in some woods by a creek with other homeless people, some relatives and some not. He said they were sending the children to knock on doors and beg for food. A relative wrote from California and said if he came out, there was work. He said they had a son nearly 2 years old and his wife was pregnant and he wanted to wait until the baby was born before they left but his wife insisted they go. He said his wife had the eyes and she had the Sight. She said if they waited, it would be too late so they left Kentucky and started West. He said they got this far and she went into labor. He wanted to get a doctor but he couldn't leave her and she told him it was no use. She said she had known for months she was going to die when the baby was born. They had hardly any money and she told him to leave her body in the church and me too. She told him some good people would adopt me and raise me. He said he believed her but all these years later he still felt guilty and he had come to see for sure I was alright.

"He also told me he was dying of cancer but I had a brother two years older who was settled with some good people out in California."

She stopped and I said, "Forrest has gone looking for your family."

"He didn't say that but I think so."

Later that evening at home, Glen talked about what happened in court. He said the judge asked about how he married Pam when he was not Sue Ellen's father. "He told me that because Pam lied to me, the marriage could be annulled. Then he talked to Pam and she objected. So I told him I just wanted it over with and Pam had agreed to an uncontested divorce and I was fine with that."

I said, "It's not that unusual. If two people marry and one of them has seriously lied to the other one over something which would have caused the other party to quite possibly not have married them, then that's grounds for an annulment. Pam telling you the baby was yours when she knew it wasn't, or even knowing it possibly wasn't, provides grounds for annulment. For people who belong to a church that forbids or discourages remarriage, it can be important."

Glen sighed. "I know she lied to me and has given me a lot of grief, but if I get to keep Sue Ellen, then it's worth it."

We were both silent for a minute and then Glen said, "I didn't expect Forrest's family to be . . . so involved." Glen added reluctantly, "They seem like nice people."

"They are," I said, "and I don't think they are going to try to take Sue Ellen away from you." I paused and then added, "They would like to share her and extra family is always good for a child. When my grandmother died, I was 12, but I sure would have liked to have had another grandmother. Sue Ellen only has you and Granny. What if you both got killed in an accident like your parents?"

Glen grimaced. "I couldn't believe it when Jimmy showed me those books Forrest wrote. Who would have believed he wrote children's stories?"

I smiled. "I know. Here he is, above six feet tall with a beard and long hair, always wearing camos and packing a gun." I shook my head. "I've been reading them again now that I know who wrote them. I'm finding they have levels in them making them interesting for adults too."

"You knew about them!" he said.

"I understand it's sort of private knowledge. His nephews wouldn't know that. His wife illustrated them and the first time I went out to his place, I recognized the illustrations."

I found my set of books. Glen looked them over and said, "I still can't believe it."

I said, "Read them. I think it may help you understand Forrest better."

That night I spent a long time on my knees. I thanked God for the day in court and its outcome. I knew God hated divorce but with Pam how she was, what else could Glen do? I prayed for Glen and Sue Ellen.

I prayed for Forrest and again, I put my heart before God and said, "Your will be done."

Chapter 15: Court Again

The next day, Glen was clearly more relaxed and more focused at the same time. He sat with Sue Ellen, as he had seen me do, and read with her, pointing to each word as it was said. Granny was running the antique store and after dealing with the one couple who had stayed overnight, I took over the general store, telling Glen to go spend some time with his daughter.

It was a peaceful day and that evening we had only one couple. Granny went to bed early and Glen came and sat at the kitchen table with me where I was on my computer. He said, "Dria, can we talk?"

I smiled and closed up my computer. "What's on your mind?" My Sight wasn't working that evening.

He said, "Will you marry me?"

I thought frantically about what to say. I liked Glen. He was a good man. I didn't want to hurt him. I couldn't think what to say.

When I didn't answer him, he sighed and said, "It's Forrest, isn't it?"

I said, "I'm not sure. I'm confused myself. Right from the beginning, I told myself to stay away from him but things just kept happening. I'm only 20. Maybe it's just a teenage crush, although I've never had one before. Maybe I'm just late developing. I don't know." I stopped and thought about what I had just said and felt like a fool.

Glen said, "So you and he have never discussed anything?"

I smiled. "We've not only never discussed anything, we've never even said anything romantic to each other." Then I paused debating whether to tell Glen. But if he understood how it was with Forrest, it would help. "Forrest told me regretted his affair with Pam and he had resolved to never kiss a woman again unless he planned to marry her."

"You admire him," Glen said.

"I admire you too," I said. "You continued to love and care for Sue Ellen even after you realized she couldn't possibly be yours."

"You're so good with Sue Ellen. She would like having you for a mother."

"And you would choose a wife in order to give Sue Ellen a good mother," I countered.

"Well," he said, and I saw he was rubbing his arm, "I do find you a very attractive woman."

I smiled. "And now you've said something much more romantic to me than Forrest has ever said."

He smiled back at me and said, "I'll take you for walks in the moonlight and Amish buggy rides if you like."

I had to laugh. I said, "Let's give it some time. This thing I have right now for Forrest will probably blow over. It's not like I've seen all that much of him. Romance is often more imagination than reality. If I spend much time with him, it may all disappear."

"In that case, I hope he does come home."

The next day, my Uncle Tom called Granny. I was being summoned to court next week on Wednesday in Bakersfield, California. Although Uncle Tom had not told Granny exactly how much I was worth, he had given me access to a bank account. I decided to fly and I wanted to take Granny with me. Uncle Tom had said he wanted her if I could possibly talk her into it.

Granny's friend, Vergie, and her granddaughter were willing to come stay while we were gone. They arrived before Granny and I left so I met them. Vergie was 78, a small bird-like old lady with bright eyes and a lively personality. She and her granddaughter had been gone on a trip to Washington, DC and had missed our Grand Opening. Now Vergie took it all in with excited interest. Her granddaughter trailed around with her and didn't say much but looked pleased with her grandmother's enthusiasm. The granddaughter was called Alice and had red hair and brown eyes. She was slightly plump but pretty and taught kindergarten at Ellsinore. As I met her, I had a picture. I saw her sitting at the picnic table behind the store teaching a red-headed child to read. The child was hers and Glen's. I smiled. It was possible.

Gloria and her mother were both willing to work while we were gone. With the Amish women doing their part, we could go.

Granny had never flown. We drove to Springfield and left my car with a college friend of Glen's who took us to the airport. Granny's enthusiasm over the new experience turned what could have been a boring trip into a lot of fun. People could not help responding to her excitement and we were even given a glimpse into the cockpit which I understand almost never happens anymore.

Uncle Tom was staying with Justin Schwartz and they were putting Granny and I up too, providing we didn't mind sharing a room. We laughed and told them about sharing the downstairs bedroom with Sue Ellen while Granny's ankle recovered.

Uncle Tom held a trustee's meeting while I went to visit Regina's family. They were happy to see me and I had a good time catching up on everyone. The house was in its usual state of homey disorder which I loved. They were more concerned with people than with things being tidy. They told me Regina was coming home on a visit next spring. She wanted to become a nun but would be sent home on six months leave and told to consider whether she was ready to commit her life to serving the poor and dying in Calcutta. I wanted to make sure I saw her while she was home.

Uncle Tom had explained to me that a number of charges and lawsuits had been filed connected to my kidnapping but the first one up in court was the lawsuit against Belle. He said if we got a conviction on this then Belle would probably plea bargain everything else but if we didn't win this one, then we were might lose them all. He thought her defense was going to claim she did not understand handling money and blame it all on the lawyer, Jake Carson, once a friend of my father's and originally one of my trustees. And later, Carson would blame it all on Belle. It was well-known tactic.

He said Belle's lawyer had manipulated the court dates to let this lawsuit come up first. He grinned and said, "He thinks Belle will make a good impression on the jury." His chuckle told me he was going to enjoy the fight which he thought we would win.

Granny talked to me. She said, "I had no idea how much money was in your father's estate. Here you turned up at our door with thirty-seven dollars and needing a job, but your father had left you several million. And he left your step-mother a nice house, a nice car, and a million dollars in a trust fund but she wants yours too." Granny was shaking her head.

I said, "I really don't want people knowing how much it is. My father always gave to the church and to missions and to charity but when people know you have money, all the wrong ones come begging for a handout." My father had secretly paid Regina's way to go on her missions trip to Calcutta and arranged for her to receive a very modest sum every month when she went back.

Granny said, "And a pretty thing like you would have all kinds of horrible men lined up at your door asking to marry you." I nodded in agreement.

The proceedings started Wednesday morning with opening arguments. The jury had already been chosen. Since this was a lawsuit, T. John Eddingham handling it. He had an impressive number of helpers buzzing around him. Uncle Tom said it mostly for show to let the jury know the importance of the case.

It really was not considered a big deal from a legal point of view. Witnesses were not being kept sequestered in the back somewhere.

T. John did his opening argument. He was good, very good. He didn't overdo the pathos and he was clear about Belle's scheming. He talked about Belle's relationship with Jake Carson and alleged it was her leading him down the path to crime, not the other way around.

Belle's lawyer was from Los Angeles and he was dramatic. He portrayed poor Belle as an innocent widow trying to do her best for a difficult and rebellious step-daughter and then being taken advantage of by a devious lawyer. It made a good story. The problem was it was not anywhere near the truth. But Belle had dressed in discrete navy for the the court hearing, even wearing a hat. She dabbed her eyes at all the right places in the tale. I wondered if they rehearsed for it, like a play.

Granny had helped me choose what to wear. It was a softly feminine blue-green dress which went with my eyes. It had a jacket and I looked young, modest, and innocent. I wore a tiger's eye necklace and bracelet Uncle Tom had brought me once from his travels. I had gotten my hair cut and styled so it spilled nicely across my shoulders, neither too stiff nor too chaotic.

I was first on the stand. We had not actually rehearsed but we had gone through what we should do. When I was called to the stand, Granny made a small show of sending a child off to something she didn't really want to do, patting me for reassurance. It wasn't really playacting and I did feel reassured. I knew she was praying for me.

T. John had gotten an artist into the courtroom who would be doing sketches which would be published in the local newspaper along with our photos taken as we entered and left court. I was portrayed that day as young and sweet looking. Later when my step-mother testified, she was drawn in her widows weeds dabbing at her eyes but somehow at the same time she was looking out sideways in a way which made her took sneaky. It was so cleverly done, I found myself almost feeling sorry for her. I knew the uninformed public reading the paper would never suspect T. John was paying the artist.

T. John took me through my story. He asked me how I would characterize my father's marriage to Belle. I said, "On the surface, it was peaceful. Father was always polite and I never heard him raise his voice to Belle. But they had very little in common and he didn't spend much time with her."

"Did he ever talk about a divorce?"

"No," I said. "My father was a good Christian man. I don't think he ever thought about a divorce."

"Did you want him to divorce her?"

"No," I answered. "It never even occurred to me. I was busy. I went to school. I worked. I was out of the house a lot. I never thought about a divorce."

"Did you and your step-mother argue?"

"No," I said. "Not until after my father died and we really didn't argue then. I just refused to sign the papers she wanted me to sign. She yelled and ranted at me but I just said 'excuse me' and left."

T. John said, "Oh, after your father died, your step-mother wanted you to sign some papers which you didn't want to sign. What were these papers about?"

"Mostly I don't know because she wouldn't let me read them."

"She wouldn't let you read them?" T. John projected his incredulous disbelief nicely. He turned and looked at the jury and repeated, "Mrs. Davis would not let her step-daughter read the papers she wanted the girl to sign!"

He turned back to me and said, "Do you have any idea what any of them were about?"

I nodded. "I did see part of the very first one. It was something about adding her signature to something. I had picked up the pen to sign but when I started to read it, I put the pen down and was going to read it carefully but Belle snatched it away. She got really mad so I just said quietly I was not going to sign it and I left the house."

T. John then went into more details: how many times did Belle try to get me to sign things? what about Jake Carson? and so on. It was all very slow and time consuming. My father said one problem lawyers had was jurors going to sleep during trials. I could see why it might happen.

I was on the stand all day. After lunch, I saw T. John had some tricks for keeping the jurors awake. At one point, after one elderly man had gone to sleep several times, T. John said, "Your honor, Juror Number 7 seems to have some kind of health problem preventing him from staying awake during these proceedings. I would like to suggest he be allowed to go home and take a nap while the number 1 alternate takes his place." The number 1 alternate was a young black man who had been following everything with keen interest.

T. John told me later, "You can't influence an audience who isn't listening." I thought about teaching preschoolers and agreed.

Thursday morning, we went on. We got to the part about me being picked up by Jeff and Loretta Cruse and being rescued by Forrest Hunter and his friends. That definitely had everyone's attention.

When T. John finished with me, then Belle's lawyer had his turn to question me. T. John had warned me to always think before I spoke and answer everything slowly. He had given me a repertoire of things to say. He said the real trick was to keep my voice calm. If the man shouted at me, I could act intimidated, shocked, or incredulous over what was said or alleged, but to never act angry.

The lawyer kept circling back to the issue of drug use. T. John had warned me he would. T. John had said, "If something is said enough times, then people tend to believe it."

At one point, I finally turned to the judge and said, like a sweet child, "I feel like I'm being badgered." The judge told him to back off.

At the end of the day, I went home wrung out. We went out to the Rice Bowl and then Justin's wife took Granny and I shopping.

The next day was Friday and T. John put my former boss at the church daycare on the stand as a character witness. She testified I had worked up to the day I called her saying I had to quit. She said I had been an exemplary employee, always on time, always pleasant, good with the children, and well-liked by her other staff. She was very sure I was not a drug user.

Belle's lawyer tried to rattle her testimony by asking her how much experience she had with detecting drug users. He had not done his homework. The woman was a volunteer worker at a homeless shelter. He backed out and dismissed her.

T. John called Jeff Cruse. I was surprised. Jeff told how Belle Davis and her lawyer had hired them to retrieve her step-daughter who was on drugs so she could put her in a re-hab center. He explained how from time to time they were hired by parents to track down children who were on drugs or in cults.

T. John asked, "So you have done this a number of times before?"

"I checked our records. In the last five years, we've done this four times, not counting Miss Davis."

"So you considered this case to be routine?"

"Fairly."

"Did it proceed in a normal manner?" T. John asked.

"Up to a certain point. There in Missouri, Miss Davis had been staying with a woman known as Granny Davis. We located her and picked her up easily and started back to Bakersfield with her. Out in the desert the other side of Mojave, we were stopped by some Marines. They were friends of Granny Davis and she was there too. They had come to get Miss Davis."

T. John did a great job with the dramatics on that one. "You mean this Granny Davis actually got the Marines to come take Miss Davis out of your custody!"

Jeff Cruse grinned. "Sure did."

T. John said, "That must have been interesting."

Jeff Curse shook his head. "More like embarrassing," he said, "but in a way I was relieved. I had begin to wonder about Miss Davis." T. John gave him time to go on. "She didn't act like a druggie. Bail jumpers are often druggies so I've seen a lot of them and she didn't act like one."

"You've seen a lot of druggies and you were thinking Miss Davis was not a druggie. Exactly why were you thinking this?"

"Well," Jeff said, "it's a long drive from Missouri to California and she wasn't getting any drugs while we had her so she should have been showing signs of withdrawal and she wasn't. What's more, she was acting real normal. She even ate normal and I've never see a druggie who ate normal."

"So based on your considerable experience with drug addicts, you don't think Miss Davis is a drug user?"

"I'm sure she's not." Jeff was clear and emphatic. T. John let the silence set for a minute and then turned to the Belle's attorney and said, "Your turn."

The defense tried hard to make Jeff look stupid and inept but failed. When we finally left at the end of the day, I thought the jury probably believed him.

It was Friday night and we took Granny to the Crystal Palace for dinner. Buck Owens was performing that night. She liked the music, although she said she preferred bluegrass. She disapproved of the alcohol but we didn't see anyone actually drunk. The food was great and she found it highly entertaining. She said, "If I lived here, I'd probably come once in a while."

Saturday we took Granny up to Sequoia National Park. She was enthralled. She said, "We've got to bring Sue Ellen some time."

The next morning, we all went to the Baptist Church which I had attended all my life. People greeted me with enthusiasm and asked me about getting rescued by the Marines. I asked how they knew about it and they said it was in the newspaper and was even mentioned on the news on Friday evening. I was surprised. But then I saw Uncle Tom wasn't.

Everyone at church thought Granny was really my grandmother and I didn't try to untangle the confusion but wondered why they didn't remember my father's mother who had been a part of this congregation until she died eight years ago.

Uncle Tom and I talked about it later and he said most people are not good at putting scattered facts together. He said, "A part of what lawyers do is line the facts up in a row so everyone can see how they fit together."

I checked the newspaper. I found photos and sketches and a headline saying, "Heiress Rescued by Marines."

Monday morning T. John put Granny on the stand. First he asked her about my character and she also was adamant that I was not a drug user. Then he asked her about the kidnapping.

She told it all, how she had asked Forrest Hunter for help, how they found me, and stopped the jeep at Four Corners.

Belle's lawyer was nice to Granny. I think he was reluctant to be seen being rough on an old lady. He did ask her how much experience she had with detecting drug users. She said, "Hemp grows wild in Missouri and all my life I've known about people smoking it." She added, "There's another thing or two out there that'll give someone a high as well." Then she said when they first hired me, I had been with her twenty-four hours a day, even sleeping in the same room. "Dria could never have been doing drugs without me knowing it."

Then the lawyer asked, "What about this James Forrest Hunter? Is he here in court?"

"No," Granny said, "he's doing some traveling but his grandmother told us she could find him if we needed him." Then Granny grinned at him. "Do you want us to find him?"

The lawyer said, "We'll see if it's necessary." I thought to myself he really didn't want Forrest in the courtroom. Why? T. John had not tracked him down either and I thought it was because he thought Forrest would not make a favorable impression on the jury. Maybe Belle's lawyer had done a little research and was afraid he'd make too much of an impression on the jury.

After Granny, T. John called Forrest's Marine buddy. After all the preliminaries, T. John took him through the 'recovery operation,' as Sarge called it. Then T. John asked, "Why were you so willing to jump in and get involved in something like this just on Mr. Hunter's say-so?"

Sarge said, with perfectly straight face, "I served with Hunter out in the middle-east. He kept us all alive more than once. He'd give us warnings and he was always right."

"Always?"

"Yes. He could smell trouble."

"So when Mr. Hunter asked you to conduct this operation, you were willing? What if it had turned out that Miss Davis had been arrested on a legitimate warrant?"

"Hunter knows people. He had checked and there was no warrant out for the girl. He said maybe the people who picked her up thought there was. We were real careful not to hurt anyone and to give them a chance to explain themselves."

"How did you pick out the right vehicle?"

"When Miss Davis was kidnapped, she had a small child with her. The child had given a description of the vehicle and the people."

"An accurate description?"

"Yes."

Belle's lawyer tried to make Sarge look like a crazy vigilante but Sarge just calmly answered his questions, including, "What would you have done if someone started shooting?"

Sarge said, "That would have been awkward since our weapons were not loaded but Hunter had brought us a couple of tasers. But our description of the vehicle was good enough that it was the only one we stopped."

That evening the newspaper printed a sketch of Sarge looking brave and trustworthy. There was also one of Granny looking sweet, alert, and grandmotherly.

Wednesday morning, T. John called Uncle Tom to the stand. He gave some complicated testimony about the money. T. John did a competent job of making it clear. A handwriting expert was called to verify forgery.

To my surprise, Belle's lawyer did not have questions for either witness.

Then T. John called Jake Carson to the stand. There was some discussion up at the judge's bench over this but he was put on the stand. His story line was he had no idea Belle was lying to him. When she said I was on drugs, he believed her. When she said I was stealing from her, he believed her. He knew nothing about the forged signatures. He gave papers to Belle and she brought them back signed.

I knew he was lying but I also knew it might could not be proved. Bell's lawyer certainly tried.

T. John rested our case. We had run overtime and we were quickly dismissed for the day. The next morning, Belle's lawyer started on her defense. She was the first witness and did a lovely job of playing the distraught widow left with a difficult step-child. She invented scenes which never happened and came across as sweet and helpless. She was on the stand all day.

T. John had made notes listing every scene and the next morning when he took over, he asked her about other witnesses. She dabbed at her eyes and said, "No." She sighed artfully and said, "I see now she was being very clever but I never thought of having to prove this in court."

T. John said, "I think someone is being very clever and it's not Miss Davis."

Belle wept and I wondered if she had onion juice in her hanky.

Belle blamed the forgeries on Jake Carson and said she had no idea he was playing games with money.

A bank employee was called to verify it was Jake Carson who dealt with the bank. But Carson had already explained Belle had always sent him to the bank and he had no idea the signatures on the papers were not legitimate.

T. John had been sharply sarcastic about that. He had said, "You're a lawyer and you didn't see what was going on?"

But Belle was such an appealing witness, so sweet and helpless. I wondered how many of the jurors would believe her.

When the case went to the jury, Granny said, "Time to pray." We prayed.

Chapter 16: Going Home

The jury didn't return a verdict until late the next afternoon but it was "Guilty." The judge reminded Belle she was out on bail and said a court date would be set for her sentencing later.

We went to the Rice Bowl again. Granny had loved it. We discussed the trial. T. John said he had already been told about the young black alternate juror being one of the keys to a guilty verdict. He was a young pastor and he told the other jurors he was sure the testimonies about me not being a druggie were right. T. John declared, "Everyone thinks young black men know all about drug use but that's not always true. However, in this case because of his work, the man does know and he convinced the others."

He said Jeff Cruse was another key to winning the case. His certainty about I was not a druggie also carried weight. T. John said, "Once the jury was convinced that the allegation of drug use was false, they didn't believe anything else Belle Davis said."

"What will happen to Belle?" I asked, thinking about my father's killer still being out on bail.

T. John said, "She still has her part of your father's estate. She may get a short prison term but it's more likely she will be given a lot of community service time. I'm sure Jake Carson has dumped her." T. John smiled. "I told him we might not pursue prosecuting him if he gave a favorable testimony. He's a snake of course and they both were just as guilty. His license to practice law in in jeopardy but I expect he'll squeak by. Nobody really expects honesty out of a lawyer."

Granny said, "So what lies did you tell during this trial?"

T. John smiled, "One was that you're a sweet innocent old lady."

Granny laughed.

Granny and Uncle Tom went with me to pack up what I had left behind when I fled to Missouri. I had made an appointment but Belle was not at home which was wise on her part. She had cleaned out my room. Nothing I had left behind was there. Fortunately, I had taken everything really important with me but I would have liked to have had my school yearbooks, report cards, things like that.

My father had had a lot of photo albums from when my mother and grandmother were still alive. After he married Belle, he had packed them up and stored them at his office. He had moved the sketch I had made of Grandmother to his office where it overlooked his desk. I went to retrieve them.

After we had moved out of the apartment over Dad's offices, he had asked the older widow who worked for him to move in with her divorced daughter and grandson. It became part of her salary. She took me to the room where the albums were stored as well as a lot more boxes. She said, "When your step-mother was getting rid of your things, I heard about it from her maid. Belle was donating them to the Salvation Army and I gave them a good donation for them. I told them what Belle was doing was probably illegal and I didn't want them to get in trouble for it."

Justin Schwartz was moving into Dad's office and was employing Mrs. Wheeler. He was picking up quite a number of my father's old clients and needed more staff. Jake Carson had been offered the office right at the beginning but had thought the location was not prestigious enough.

Granny and I were headed home. I bought a small pick-up truck with a simple camper shell which we thought we could easily drive. Regina's brothers had arranged it. They had a car repair business. They made a shelf of plywood to go in the camper shell to hold a mattress. The shelf was hinged so things could be stored under it. They told us it was a fairly common arrangement for that sort of camper shell.

I sorted through all my things and packed some boxes including

Dad's photo albums and my sketch of Grandmother. We put them under the plywood shelf in the back of the truck. Most of my boxes had been filled with books. I had chosen some favorites but gave the rest to Mrs. Wheeler who was pleased to get a library for her grandson.

Granny and I set off on a road trip. Granny said she had always wanted to see the Grand Canyon. We also saw cliff dwellings, a pueblo, the painted desert, the petrified forest, and a huge meteor crater. We parked in campgrounds, rest stops, and truck stops. One night when it was cold and rainy, we got a motel room. It took us seven days to get home. We had fun.

Along the way, Granny talked to me about Glen. She said, "He told me he was going to ask you to marry him. I'd love to have you in the family but I wasn't surprised when you told him you weren't really ready to make a choice."

I said, "No, I'm only 20 and I've never really dated anyone."

"I haven't wanted to ask you about this Second Sight thing. Do you really have it?"

I told Granny, "Sometimes. It's on and off. Forrest's grandmother said as you get older, you get better at knowing what you're seeing. I hope so. She also said a Sighting is not set in stone. You can do things to change it and so can other people." I paused and then said, "She said if I saw something which was a danger to someone, then I should warn them. But she said if it was other things, to stay out of people's lives and let them live without the burden of predictions."

"So Forrest's grandmother has it."

I realized I had revealed personal knowledge I hadn't intended to tell but there was no taking it back. "Yes," I answered her.

"And Forrest."

It was not a question. I said, "I think it tortures him. He didn't see when his wife and son were going to be shot."

Granny nodded. "He's a tortured man." Then she said, "You love him."

Again, it wasn't a question but I answered as though it were. "I'm not sure. I really tried to stay away from him but things kept happening. When he finally found out about Sue Ellen and he and Glen fought, I followed him home to talk to him. I knew somehow we connect. I don't know how it happened but I'm attached to him."

Granny said, "I think you interested him from the very first time he saw you. When he came to help with cleanup, he asked about you. And then he kept coming around and I don't think it was just me he was interested to see."

"I thought I would give things some time and see what happens," I told her and Granny nodded.

We arrived home late on a Saturday evening. Sue Ellen was in bed but the adults were up. We exchanged news. Glen's transfer to Ellsinore was finalized. The business was running smoothly and we had three rooms occupied tonight.

The next morning when Vergie and Alice were leaving, Glen and Sue Ellen both seemed reluctant to see them go. I noticed and smiled.

Later I asked Sue Ellen if she had had fun with Alice. She said, "Yes," and got another book from her room and read it to me.

We went to church and it was Johnathan Underwood, the young preacher who had come home with us the day Ray and Pam had done their vandalism. He was friendly and asked if he was scheduled to go home with us again. He wasn't and he expressed regret and said he would drop by the store before he went home today.

I explained the store was not open on Sundays and he obviously was astonished. I carefully kept a straight face but I privately thought it was hilarious. It was the absurdity of it. He was supposed to be an advocate of keeping the Sabbath but was surprised to find people doing it.

Then he asked if he might drop by for a visit later. I said, "Granny might like that. She likes to talk religion and the man she usually does it with is gone right now."

I knew very well the young preacher did not want to drop by and discuss religion with Granny but I was feeling just little bit ornery and he was so stuffy, I couldn't resist.

He said, "I was hoping you and I might get better acquainted."

I tried to think of something tactful to say but what I was thinking was, *Oh, glory! Just what I need right now – another man.* I finally said, "If you come by on a Sunday, ring the bell on the door to the general store. There's a dog around back who objects to people she doesn't know."

"How did those vandals get in?" he asked.

"It was Ray Williams and his sister, Pam. Pam is Glen's ex-wife and Sue Ellen's mother. She used to live there."

He was shocked. But it didn't scare him off. I sent Glen to let him in. I offered him coffee and cake and he accepted. Granny told me quietly before he arrived about the local papers carrying the story about me and she knew people at church had told him. She said, "He was interested in you before and he's a minister so maybe he really isn't after your money."

Granny asked him how his studies were going and when he gave a short, vague answer, she asked him what was his favorite subject. He floundered around before finally saying he liked studying Greek and Hebrew. Granny said she had a big concordance with Greek and Hebrew and found it quite interesting to track a word around to get its flavor in the original language.

Sue Ellen woke up and I went to get her, although usually Glen did this when he was not busy. He followed me up the stairs. "He's down there asking Granny for suggestions as to what there is to see in the area. I think he wants to take you somewhere."

"I think I'll exit via the guest hallway."

Glen said, "How can we get rid of him?"

I got an idea. We went back down the stairs together. I took Sue Ellen on through to the kitchen for milk and cake at the table while Glen stopped in the living room and asked the young preacher what he thought of divorce.

Since he knew about Glen's divorce, he tried to give a tactful answer. He said, "Well, normally I'm opposed to it but I do realize that sometimes it's unavoidable."

Glen plowed straight ahead. "And what about re-marriage? Some people are telling me I am not free to remarry but my daughter needs a mother and I've been trying to talk Dria into marrying me."

The poor man flapped around and I wished I'd had a tape recorder handy. He first said something and then contradicted himself and backtracked and then started talking about Jesus and the woman caught in adultery, although what that had to do with it wasn't clear. His confusion and lack of clarity was humorous.

He finally excused himself and left.

Granny said, "Glen, did you think of that or did Dria put you up to it?" I confessed my guilt and Granny laughed. Then she said, "I shouldn't laugh but the poor man was so discombobulated." Then she shook her head and said, "If the man is going to be a preacher, he's going to have to learn to deal with questions like those."

Later that day, I took Sue Ellen outside while Glen and Granny were looking at the accounts for the business. Then Glen came out. I was sketching Sue Ellen again. He asked if I would do a sketch for him to be framed.

Then he said, "Granny told me she warned you the paper printed things about you while you were gone. Here's the main article from the Poplar Bluff paper." The headline said, "Oil Heiress Kidnapped at Local Flea Market." The details were mostly accurate, too accurate. Everyone would know who I was and where I lived – and that I was worth several million dollars.

I read it through, looked at Glen, and said, "I'm tempted to cuss."

"I couldn't believe it and I asked Granny if it was true. She said to talk to you."

When he didn't say anything else, I said, "Glen, I know you are not after my money."

He said, "I can see why you keep quiet about it."

I said, "Yes, it would attract the wrong men." I paused and then added, "And keep good men from even trying."

He turned and looked at me sharply and then said, "I guess that's true too."

I smiled. I said, "I actually don't get it until next April when I turn 21."

"What are you going to do?"

"Stay right here with you and Granny and Sue Ellen. I know none of you are after my money and I like it here."

Glen said, "School starts in two weeks. I've picked up my textbooks and need to get prepared. Mrs. Carter who is retiring has been helpful but I've realized she had not been very innovative."

I said, "Innovative can be good but traditions develop when ways of doing things work."

Glen laughed. "Where did you get that one?" he asked.

"One of my teachers at college. One student complained about her classes being boring. Our instructor said teaching pre-schoolers was often boring and if someone wanted excitement, they should choose another profession. Then one of the other students told us her brother was a fire fighter and he said it was long stretches of intense boredom punctuated by episodes of intense fear."

We laughed and Glen said, "Dria, I really do like you."

I said, "I know and I like you but I'm not the only fish in the pond." However, Glen seemed unaware and I thought maybe something had happened to change the picture I had seen of Alice.

While Granny and I were gone to California, Glen had gotten a call from Pam. She had asked again for money. She threatened to change her mind about custody because now she knew Forrest was letting Glen keep Sue Ellen. Glen said he thought about getting a loan to pay her but decided to talk to Forrest's lawyer first to see if Pam actually could change her mind.

The lawyer told Glen he would deal with Pam. He said if Pam ever contacted him again or showed her face here, he wanted us to let him know immediately. He told Glen that Pam was out of jail on bail but had not shown up for her court date so her bail had been revoked and a warrant put out for her arrest.

He also told Glen to take Granny and go to the courthouse in Van Buren and file for something called an *ex parte* order. The lawyer said they could do this because of the vandalism incident. Then if she showed up here, law enforcement could arrest her immediately.

Glen said, "I got the idea from the lawyer that Pam had been given money by someone. Did you do that?"

"No," I told him, "but Forrest might have. In court when I heard about Pam signing her parental rights over to Forrest, it occurred to me he might have paid her off."

Glen looked puzzled. "If he paid Pam off, why was he willing to leave Sue Ellen with me?"

"Because he cares about Sue Ellen. You heard what the lawyer said he said. He does care. His sister's kids have talked about him quite a bit. He likes kids and I think he understands them."

Glen looked at me. "But how did he know what kind of a parent I am? From you?"

"Maybe," I said. But I wondered if Forrest had also had a Sighting.

I thought about Pam. I thought about how my father's killer was still running around loose. It was consistent with Pam's character to sell the child. When she was arrested, she was high on cocaine. If Pam got her, Sue Ellen would end up being terribly abused. And it would be just like her to demand more money in the future. I found myself thinking about taking action. If Glen did something, he'd end up in jail. If I did it, who would suspect? I was not related. I started thinking how I could do it. If she disappeared and I withdrew a sum of money from an account and said I paid her off and she told me she was going to Mexico, would anyone really investigate?

Then I realized what I was seriously planning was murder. Then I said to myself, *Not murder – execution.* I started praying. I started praying earnestly.

School started and we settled into a new routine of Glen being gone all day on week days. Gloria's mother was happy to oblige when we needed her. Fall harvest was underway and Sofie wasn't coming much but she did show up on many Saturdays. The buggy rides were bringing in enough money to make it well worth it. Tourist travel had slowed some and it was more older people but Saturdays were busy. Granny said the tourist traffic would continue until late October.

Older people liked our bed and breakfast and we had gotten leery of renting rooms to young people. While Granny and I were in California, Glen had had to evict a wild party. He had used the shot gun. When the law arrived, the pot smokers had tried to file charges against him because of the gun. In the end, it was agreed they would not be charged with marijuana possession if they paid their bill, including cleaning charges, and quietly left. Glen said he overheard one of the sheriff's deputies telling them they better not try to take revenge because Glen knew how to use that shotgun.

I worked on formatting my book which was far more tedious and time consuming than I ever could have imagined. My sketches to illustrate it were out at Forrest's place. He had said he would scan them and we could integrate them into the book but he had not given them to me yet when he left.

Sue Ellen's fourth birthday arrived. We had a quiet little celebration. Her problem with her r's had suddenly cleared up and she was growing. I saw already she was going to have the tall, lanky physique of Forrest's family. Glen was not overweight but his build was stockier.

We arranged a Sunday with Forrest's family. The grandmothers set it up. They told Glen that putting out the kinship story would stop people from making awkward speculations. So we all went to church with Forrest's family and then had a picnic on the deck at his parent's house. After that, all of us but the two grandmothers piled into canoes and paddled down to Big Spring. I had never canoed before but Glen had. We had Sue Ellen in our canoe in a life jacket and I wore one too. I can swim but not well. Our party formed a fleet of five canoes. I learned the best paddler was always put in the back. Each of the boys' parents and grandparents was in the back of a canoe with a boy in the front. Mary Ellen was in the center of a canoe with her father at the back and Jimmy at the front. I was amazed at what a lovely activity canoeing is. It was a great day and I saw Glen gradually relax when no one was focused on Sue Ellen.

Forest's mother, Jenny, told me quietly with no one else around, "I notice Sue Ellen's r's have surfaced. Jay was just the same. He'd also had trouble with his s's. I was considering a speech therapist when suddenly around his fourth birthday, it all disappeared." I didn't say anything. The poignant look in Jenny's eyes made me realize just how much she would have enjoyed watching Sue Ellen develop.

The boys had talked casually about going canoeing with Uncle Jay but otherwise, Forrest wasn't discussed.

That night when I prayed, I found myself praying for him but with nothing like the urgency I had felt when he first left. I had much more of a sense of peace but it was not a Sighting. I prayed for Glen and his new job and also for his future.

Chapter 17: Winter

As Granny had predicted, the tourist traffic slowed down and we fell into a routine with different women coming mid-morning, helping while we cleaned rooms and staying through the lunch crowd. Gloria's mother continued to come all day on Fridays. Granny said she needed the income. She did a lot of the serious cleaning and even some painting. I had time for Sue Ellen and her reading was progressing rapidly.

One Saturday a few weeks after the canoeing expedition, Forrest's family all came over. It was a fine day and the children went out back to play. I sat at the picnic table and sketched. Jimmy came to look and said, "Wow, you're good. Our Aunt Ella was an artist. I remember her but my younger brothers don't really."

"I've seen some of your Aunt Ella's work out at your uncle's house."

Jimmy nodded. "I wish Uncle Jay would come home. He takes us on hikes and teaches us all about the plants and animals. Did you know that you can tell if a snake is poisonous or not just by looking at its head?"

I didn't.

Jimmy said poisonous snakes have cheeks wider than their necks because of their poison glands. If the head is the same width as the neck, then it isn't a poisonous snake. He added, "They can still bite you and it would hurt but you wouldn't die from it."

Jimmy sighed. "Uncle Jay has a cave on his place and he took Joe and I caving once. He said the others were still too young."

Then Jimmy asked, "Did you really get kidnapped?"

I said, "Sort of."

"I wasn't trying to eavesdrop but Mom and Dad were talking about it and didn't know I was there. They told me not to tell the other kids. They said Uncle Jay rescued you."

"Yes," I said. "In a way it was a mix-up. My step-mother told these people some lies and got them to come here and catch me and take me back to California. But your uncle and Granny figured out who had me and where they were going. So your uncle took Granny and they flew out to California. Your uncle used to be in the Marines and he got some of his old buddies to help him and they got me back."

"Wow!" Jimmy said. "Did anyone get shot?"

"No," I told him. "They were careful not to hurt anyone. If they had, they would have been in trouble."

"Why?"

"Because they were not law officers and it wasn't really their job to catch the bad guys. And my kidnappers were not really bad people. They had just been told lies."

"What kind of lies?"

"My step-mother told them I was on drugs and she wanted to help me by putting me in a drug re-hab center. So you see the people who kidnapped me thought they were helping me."

Jimmy was puzzled. "But can't they do tests to see if you're on drugs?"

"Yes," I told him, "but it takes a few days to get the answers. Actually the people who had me were beginning to suspect they'd been told lies. In the end, they were happy your Uncle Jay came and got me."

"Cinderella had a mean step-mother and so did Hansel and Gretel."

I saw where his mind was going and I said, "Not all step-mothers are mean. Abraham Lincoln had a good step-mother who encouraged him to get an education. And sometimes a real mother is mean. It does happen."

"Was Sue Ellen's mother mean?"

I hesitated and then said, "She was a bad mother but she's gone now."

Jimmy nodded. "Mary Ruth said Sue Ellen's mom and dad got a divorce. She said Sue Ellen gets to live with you and Uncle Glen and Granny. Are you and Uncle Glen getting married?"

"No, I don't think so." I told him.

"Don't you like him?" he asked.

"Yes," I said. "I do like him but getting married to someone takes a little more than liking."

"Yeah," he nodded wisely. "Falling in love. My dad said if I ever did it, to tell him immediately."

"Oh," I said, "that sounds like a good idea."

"That's exactly what Uncle Jay said," Jimmy told me. "I asked him why and he said falling in love was a kind of insanity so people in love do crazy things. He said you needed to tell someone who has good common sense and then do whatever they tell you to do."

I nodded. "That sounds like a good plan to me."

"Have you ever fell in love?" he asked.

I didn't know what to say. No wasn't true but I wasn't sure yes was either. And I certainly did not want to discuss the possibility with Forrest's 13-year-old nephew. I finally said, "I'm not sure. Maybe I need to talk to someone with good common sense and see what they tell me to do."

Jimmy sighed. "Too bad Uncle Jay isn't here. He has good common sense."

Oh, mercy, I thought. Just the idea of talking to his uncle about it had me in knots.

I was rescued by the boy's mother, Joanna. She said, "I've spent my allowance. Time to quit." She had been in the antique store. "There are some really nice things in that store and such a variety. It's a lot more interesting than a normal store."

She sat down at the picnic table beside me and looked at the sketch I had been doing of Jacob, her youngest boy. She said, "You're good. Did you know Jay's wife was an artist?"

"Yes," I told her. "That was how I figured out about Forrest being

Jay Hunter and writing those books. I saw the illustrations in his study and recognized them."

"I don't know where Jay has gone but Grandma seems to be sure he's okay. Dad says she says he hasn't called but Grandma always seems to know things."

I nodded. "She has the Sight."

"You know about that?" Joanna's voice was loaded with emotion but I wasn't sure what – fear, excitement, dismay, amazement, doubt – maybe a combination of them all.

"I know." I said.

"I thought Jay had it too but he says its not reliable. He said sometimes he knows things he doesn't want to know and then he didn't know anything when Ella and Little Jay were shot."

I wasn't sure what to say but Mary Ruth came running up to her mother to show her a bug she had found. She wanted to know it's name. Joanna didn't know. She said, "Ask your Uncle Jay when he comes home."

I realized Forrest had left a hole in other lives besides mine.

The round of young preachers continued but Johnathan Underwood didn't reappear. Granny said, "We should apologize to that young man." The tall skinny one I privately thought of as *The Stork* did reappear regularly and one Sunday we were getting him for dinner. I suggested to Granny that she invite Gloria. She looked at me and then said, "I would never have thought of that." The Stork was actually named Richard Twitter which made me smile when I heard it. I wondered if he had been teased about his name because he always introduced himself as just Brother Richard.

Gloria came and chattered happily about how she liked her contacts, and did he think he could get some? She was quite relaxed and was not slumping. I saw she had definitely gained confidence during the last months. She started talking about the Amish and their religious beliefs and she and the young preacher had quite a discussion about it. The young man was much more interesting than Jonathan

Underwood.

We moved through the winter with occasional visits back and forth with Forrest's family on Sunday afternoons. These were mostly short. They were busy and we are tied to the business and can really only leave on Sundays. Joanna and Grandma Ruth sometimes came to the antique store. They always had Mary Ruth and sometimes some of the boys but never all of them at once.

Christmas vacation came which meant the children and teachers all had time off from school. On Sunday we went over and went to church with Forrest's family. After dinner, the men and boys all went to play games down on the basement level of the house. Mary Ruth had gotten a huge doll house for Christmas which opened and came with lots of furniture and a family of dolls. She and Sue Ellen were soon very busy. Granny and Grandma Ruth went off somewhere talking about quilting and I found myself doing clean-up with Forrest's mother, Jenny, and his sister, Joanna. When we finished, we sat down at the kitchen table with coffee. Joanna said, "I love kids and I wanted a big family but sometimes I wonder if I was crazy. If I didn't have a good husband and parents who pitch in, it would be impossible."

I was told Forrest's father, James, had only had the one sister who was Down Syndrome but Jenny had come from a larger family with three siblings and lots of nieces and nephews who were now producing children. However, her parents had been military and they all lived elsewhere, one sister even in England. Her parents had settled in Arizona when they retired. She told me because she had been moved around so much growing up, she had been determined to settle somewhere and stay. She said, "With no family to help me and Grandma Ruth having to care for James' sister, I decided two kids were enough but I told Joanna to have a whole house full and I'd help her."

They never asked me about my family and I had decided it was because of the *Oil Heiress* thing. So I told them about my mother falling when I was 4 and lying helpless in a nursing home until I was 10. I told them about my grandmother dying when I was 12. I said, "My best friend came from a family of twelve kids and I loved to go over to her house."

Joanna exclaimed, "Twelve! and I thought five was a lot. Actually we planned for four but when they were all boys, we couldn't decide if we wanted more or not, but then Mary Ruth happened. We call her our bonus kid. We thought about another one but decided five was enough."

I said, "I'm not sure twelve was really planned. They're Catholic and have never said anything indicating they didn't want that many."

Jenny nodded. "I think telling a child they were not wanted is child abuse."

Joanna said, "I know. I was in the grocery store once when Jerry was a baby and I heard some woman actually tell her son she had wanted a girl and not a boy and if she could, she would have sent him back. I wanted to ask the woman if I could have him but he ran out of the store and she was cussing and upsetting Jimmy and Joe, so I left. I didn't see the boy anywhere outside and I think if I had, I'd have taken him home with me."

Jenny said, "One of the hardest things teachers ever have to deal with is child abuse situations."

Granny and Grandma Ruth returned and were discussing a quilting exhibition which was held annually over in Paducah, Kentucky. They asked Joanna if she would take them. Grandma Ruth had been several times in the past. Granny said she'd heard of it and really wanted to go.

I had hoped Forrest would come home for Christmas but he was barely mentioned so it was clear he wasn't expected. I talked to Uncle Tom a long time on the phone. I had finished formatting my book. I told Uncle Tom about the project and how I didn't want to ask Forrest's housekeeper for my sketches because I didn't want to talk to everyone here about it.

Uncle Tom told me the court case for my father's killer had again been delayed.

Then after Christmas, I got a CD in the mail. It was my sketches.

The return address was Forrest's although it had been mailed in California. There was no letter, nothing except the CD in a priority mail cardboard envelope addressed to me at the Davis General Store. The addresses had been printed onto sticky address labels.

As I held the CD in my hand, I saw Uncle Tom talking to Forrest. Forrest had no beard and his hair was cut in a short, ordinary style. I knew it was a Sighting. That night I prayed for Forrest, wondering how he and Uncle Tom had gotten together. When they met here, Forrest had said something when he left about talking again sometime. I decided Forrest had looked Uncle Tom up and Uncle Tom must have mentioned the sketches.

We were into January and had not had a good snow yet. I was disappointed. Bakersfield, California never gets snow so I was looking forward to it. But all it had done was rain, sleet, and produce snow flurries which didn't stick around. Then one night in late January, it started snowing just before dark and they were predicting six inches. About midnight, we were awakened by the bell on the store. Glen went down and came back up and said we had guests for the bed and breakfast. It was two men and Glen said he had put them in a room together which they didn't mind as it had two beds. We had not had many guests after the weather turned cold and when we did, they had usually made reservations. Glen said these two had come looking for Forrest and discovered he wasn't home.

The next morning it was still snowing and the weather forecasters were saying we might get ten inches. Our two guests appeared at a reasonable time considering how late they went to bed. They were on their way to Texas but had planned to stop and see Forrest Hunter on the way. They had served with Forrest in the middle-east. However, when they tried to phone him, they only got an answering machine. They were driving a jeep with four-wheel drive and had gotten back to Forrest's gate but the place looked deserted and no one answered the intercom. Glen told them we didn't know when Forrest would be back.

At breakfast, the two men noticed Sue Ellen's eyes. Granny told them how she and Forrest's grandmother had decided they were related. I was glad the two old ladies had come up with the story. I had discovered several Green Valley people who had previously thought Forrest was Sue Ellen's father, now believed the story the two grandmothers had circulated.

As we gave the two men breakfast, they started telling us about Hunter, as they called him. One of them said, "I swear he's half wildcat. He could smell trouble and even tell us what kind was coming. Several times we'd have all been dead if he hadn't warned us."

They also told us Forrest had invented several improvements to military equipment. "Hunter's smart," they said. "He registered the patents for them and then sold them to the manufacturing companies. He made a couple of million out of the deal."

They had planned to leave but it was still snowing and the roads had not been plowed. Someone came and Glen opened the store. Granny told him to call her if anyone wanted into the antique store. Then someone in a four-wheel drive pickup brought us a middle-aged couple who had spent the night in their car in a ditch. They rented a room, had hot baths, and we fed them. Forrest's buddies took the man and they got his car out of the ditch and to the store. It snowed all day and Granny introduced us to snow-cream and I learned how to make yeast rolls which is basically an all day affair. When the snow finally quit late afternoon, we had more than a foot. I took Sue Ellen out to play in the snow and Glen and Forrest's two buddies all joined us. We made a snowman, then a snow lady, and then some snow children. Sue Ellen asked, "Can we make a snow house?" We tried and ended up with several rooms with walls three or four feet high. Sue Ellen's enthusiasm infected us all.

Just as it was getting dark, the snow plows came through. Our guests all decided they would stay the night and leave tomorrow morning. They had all been in the antique store and bought things. Granny told me later, "We should get people stuck here more often. Between them, those four people spent more than two thousand dollars."

Forrest's friends had continued to talk about him all day. That night I prayed for him. And then as I lay in bed, I thought about the things they had told me. One of them was he had always talked about his wife. They had heard about his wife and son getting killed. One of them said, "How many men got a woman they'd just as soon not have but the one who gets killed is the one whose man would have gladly taken that bullet for her. Life ain't fair."

The next morning, they all moved on and our usual customers started appearing. The next day school restarted and life moved on. I liked it, the familiar circle of people, church on Sunday, the customers. Sue Ellen was happy. Glen seemed content. As this was his first year at Ellsinore, he had to put a lot of effort into preparation for his classes. He said next year would be much easier.

April was approaching and with it would come my twenty-first birthday. I expected I would have to go out to California to sign papers but Uncle Tom told me he was coming for a visit and bringing what needed my signature. I was surprised he could get away from the university but he said he could arrange it.

In one way I was content with my life but I knew also I was waiting for something. I was waiting for Forrest to come home.

Logically I knew he might not come home. I wasn't sure what I was going to do if he didn't. All I could do was pray and wait.

Chapter 18: My Birthday

As my birthday approached, I had my book formatted. I had edited and re-edited. I had designed the cover. I had formatted the sketches to be included. It had taken me ages to figure out how to do that. I knew I probably didn't have everything just right but I had done all I could do. I was ready to show it to Forrest.

My birthday was actually on a Saturday and Uncle Tom arrived on Friday evening. We put him in one of the spare bedrooms upstairs and the next morning we signed papers. The signings were all witnessed by Gloria's mother, Mary Miller, and Vergie's granddaughter, Alice. When Uncle Tom explained we needed witnesses who could be found later if needed, Granny had called her friend, Vergie. Mary Miller had been reluctant but Uncle Tom had been charming when he explained we needed a witness who's truthfulness could not be questioned. Afterwards, Uncle Tom spend most of the day going through things with me which I needed to know. He had made a helpful file for me.

Bakersfield, California is an oil field area and Dad had provided financing at the right time to the right people. Then he had put profits into other businesses. When oil prices were high, he had sold part of his holdings and diversified even more. I learned I now owned a small mortgage company which specialized in funding housing and small businesses. It had given Regina's family the loan to buy their house and had loaned money to two of her brothers to open a car repair business. I knew they didn't know Dad was the mortgage company.

Saturday evening we had roast with potatoes and carrots which is one of my favorite meals. Granny had made a chocolate birthday cake which had cream filling. She laughed at my surprise. The homemade ice cream freezer had its first outing of the season.

Vergie and her granddaughter had stayed for the day and I noticed Alice's eyes following Glen. When I got a chance, I said to her, "Glen is a good man and a really good father."

She looked at me and said, "He told me he asked you to marry him."

I said, "I really like him but he's not the one. I've been told that falling in love is a kind of insanity."

She responded, "Glen said he thought you were in love with someone else."

"I think so," I told her.

On Sunday Uncle Tom went to church with us and Forrest's family had been invited to our church for a change. The Stork took a look at the larger than usual congregation and produced a livelier than usual performance. Gloria, seated in front of us on the second pew with her parents, may also have provided extra inspiration. Or maybe it was his new contact lens.

As Forrest's family filed in, I caught a glimpse of an extra man, tall and beardless with a normal tidy haircut and normal tidy clothes of jeans with a blue shirt and denim vest. I knew immediately it was Forrest. However, as we settled into our usual seats along with Uncle Tom, I knew Glen had not noticed him. During the congregational singing, Forrest's whole family joined in but I could detect Forrest's voice among the others.

After church, they were invited back to our place for dinner. At the end of the service, The Stork was at the door shaking hands with everyone as they left and I saw Forrest lean over and say something in his ear as he shook hands with him. I suddenly saw a picture of The Stork with a beard, looking like an Old Testament prophet. Outside, Glen still didn't see Forrest until he moved up along side of him said, "Glen." When Glen turned to look at him, Forrest said, "May I talk to you for a minute?"

Glen didn't recognize him until he looked him squarely in the eyes and I saw the shock go through him. Forrest smiled and said, "Just a quiet friendly little talk."

I had Sue Ellen's other hand and I took her to the SUV while Glen and Forrest moved off to talk. Sue Ellen asked, "Who's that man?"

I said, "He's Mary Ruth's Uncle Jay."

"He has eyes like Mary Ruth and her Grandma."

"Yes," I said. "That's why I think he's her Uncle Jay."

"Is he my Uncle Jay?"

"I think so," I said.

I watched the two men carefully. Glen had been tense but after several minutes talk, he shook hands with Forrest and they parted. As Glen moved toward the SUV, he no longer seemed up-tight and he said, "Everyone is going to beat us home."

The afternoon was warm enough for the children to play in the sheltered back yard. Forrest was in the middle of it. He had not worn his gun into church but he had it now. His family seemed so used to it, no one commented, not even the boys.

Joanna, Billy Joe, James, Glen, and I were also all outside. Jenny came and went while Granny, Grandma Ruth, and Uncle Tom stayed inside. The boys were begging Forrest to take them on a hike in the woods. He asked me if Glen and I were willing to go so he could take the two girls also.

We set off with Forrest leading, followed by the four boys, then me with Mary Ruth followed by Glen with Sue Ellen at the end. Forrest stopped often asking the boys for the name of a tree or plant or when he spotted an insect or animal. When we came upon some daffodils in bloom, he asked the boys what their presence there meant. They didn't know. "Guess," he told them.

"But who planted them?" Jerry asked.

Forrest said, "Exactly. Who do you think planted them?"

Jimmy said, "Someone used to live here."

Forrest asked, "How do you know?"

Jimmy said, "Look. This is a rose bush." He moved a few steps up the slope and said, "I think there used to be a house here. Look." We looked at a vine covered hump which once had been a fireplace built of rocks.

Glen said, "This is the old Wallis cabin. When I was a kid, it was easier to see. It burned a long time ago."

"Did they get attacked by Indians?" Jerry asked.

Glen shook his head. "Granny says old man Wallis was drunk a lot and one night he dropped a kerosene lantern and was too drunk to get the fire out so the whole cabin burned."

It was Jimmy who said, "And that shows what can happen if you get drunk."

I saw the twinkle in Forrest's eye but he kept a straight face and solemnly agreed with the boys.

We started home but Forrest put Jimmy in charge of leading us back. Jimmy did it without hesitation and I saw he had expected his Uncle Jay to ask him to lead us back home. When we arrived, Forrest announced next time they went on a hike, it would be Joe's job to lead them home.

Glen had ended up carrying Sue Ellen before the end of the hike. Forrest said to him quietly, "Sorry. I tried not to make it too long. She would have not wanted to be left behind."

Glen nodded. "I don't mind carrying her."

I got a book to read to Sue Ellen and Mary Ruth while Forrest and Glen organized a softball game. He and Glen formed a team with Jerry and Jacob while James and Billy Joe formed a team with Jimmy and Joe. I heard Jimmy say, "Uncle Glen, this is great. With you playing, we can make even teams. Usually we have to make Mom play and she really doesn't like it much."

Sue Ellen was asleep in my lap almost immediately but I continued to read to Mary Ruth. When I finished the story, I took Sue Ellen in and put her in her crib in the downstairs bedroom. Mary Ruth followed me and after we went back out into the living room, she said, "I would like to have a little sister. Mama told me angels bring babies and I asked Jesus for one but we haven't got it yet."

I said, "Well, babies are a lot of work and maybe Jesus knows it would be too much work for your mother. Maybe you can just borrow Sue Ellen sometimes."

In the living room, I found Uncle Tom perusing a book from Granny's bookshelf. The grandmothers had gone upstairs talking about a quilt and the other women had gone outside and Mary Ruth went to join them. Through the window, I saw Forrest coaching 7-year-old Jacob on batting.

I don't know what Uncle Tom saw in my face but he put the book down and said, "I can see why you like it here."

He was sitting in the recliner Glen normally used and I went automatically to the wing-back chair where I always sat. "Forrest found you out in California."

"He said he was on a quest."

"He found his grandmother's brother, he found you, and . . . ." I paused but then voiced what else I was thinking, "and he found his faith."

"He said you . . . see things."

I smiled. "Did he? Did he tell you he sees things too."

Uncle Tom nodded. "I wasn't quite sure what to make of it all. I mostly just listened and prayed for the man. Have you made up your mind?"

"Not really," I said.

"He's likable and intelligent but also unconventional. If something doesn't make sense to him, he doesn't hesitate to rebel. His heart is in the right place but he's unpredictable."

I sighed. "A risk," I said.

"Yes," Uncle Tom said.

"And Glen is safe, predictable, steady, dependable."

"Has he said anything?"

"He asked me to marry him."

Uncle Tom sighed. "I can't choose for you."

"I know," I said. "And whatever I choose, I have to take responsibility for the consequences."

Uncle Tom smiled, "Dria, how could anyone ever believe you were taking drugs?"

I was puzzled at the *non sequitur*.

He saw my expression and said, "Taking drugs is escaping reality. You may have visions but you face reality squarely. It's that total acceptance of the real world which makes me believe in your visions."

"Oh," I said, lamely.

"Shall I pray for you?" he asked.

I smiled and said, "Please."

He moved over to put his hand on my bowed head and said, "Father God, you love Dria even more than her father did. You want what's best for her. She's facing a major decision in her life. Please show her what to do. We, with our earthy wisdom, often think we know what's best, but you with your eternal perspective, see far more. Please guide Dria's path. We ask in Jesus' Name. Amen."

I felt the in-flooding of peace in my heart and I knew it was the presence of the Holy Spirit.

I asked, tentatively, "Did Forrest say anything to you about me?"

Uncle Tom smiled. "He'll have to do his own talking."

I wandered outside to watch the softball game and found my eyes drawn again and again to Forrest. It wasn't his skill as a player. Glen and Billy Joe were both better. I saw how he was always aware of the boys, where they were, how they were progressing with their skills, and encouraging them. He was a born teacher.

Then I had a Sight. Forrest was older and the boy he was teaching was ours, his and mine. The boy I saw was only one of several children.

I sat, lost in thought, until everyone was moving around. The game was over. It was getting chilly. It was time to go in and eat.

We adults happily ate leftovers while the children found sandwiches more attractive. I tried to hide my intense interest but my eyes kept finding their way back to Forrest.

And what I noticed was he was not watching me. He was talking to people, engaged, smiling easily and involved. But he was not watching me. He was not interested in me like I was in him. I was not the one his eyes were following.

Then the boys were clamoring for Uncle Jay to do story-making with them. Glen borrowed the white board normally sat out by the door of the antique store when any booths were running sales. They organized themselves in the upstairs hall, leaving Mary Ruth and Sue Ellen to build a Lego castle on the coffee table in the living room. Again Jenny, Joanna, and I were doing clean-up.

Joanna shook her head and said, "I have tried doing story-making with them but Jay has a knack for it I just don't have." When I asked what it involved, she said, "Sneak up the stairs and listen. Mom and I can take care of this."

The boys were sitting cross-legged on the floor with Glen at the back. Forrest was standing in front by the white board on its easel. He had written in a column down the left side, "What? Who? Where? When? How? Why?"

The boys were making suggestions. A robbery at Granny's store was rejected on the grounds they had done that one before. The antique store was rejected as too similar. A murder was suggested but then who would get murdered? A bad guy. What bad guy? Then Jimmy said, "Let's do a kidnapping. Uncle Jay, you know about kidnappings."

"Who gets kidnapped?" Forrest asked him.

Jimmy knew he was not supposed to talk about my kidnapping. He thought and then said, "A little kid like Sue Ellen who's too little to tell on the kidnappers."

"Who's going to kidnap her?"

Jimmy said, "Let's make it like Sue Ellen where she lives with her dad and her mother kidnaps her."

"Why would her mother kidnap her?" Forrest asked.

"For money," Jimmy said. "She wants the father to pay her money to get the little kid back."

I could see Glen's tension. It was far too close to reality. I suspected Forrest also was uncomfortable but he went on with the game. The boys laid out a whole scenario of where and when and how the child was kidnapped. They decided where she was being kept. Then Forrest asked, "Will her father pay the ransom or will she get rescued without him paying?"

The boys wanted her rescued. They set up a plot where the child's older cousins played detective and very cleverly found out where the child was hid. They managed to rescue her, unharmed of course, and get the police to arrest the mother and her evil boyfriend.

At the end, Jimmy asked, "Uncle Jay, can I write this story down?"

"Of course," Forrest said. "Bring it to me when you've finished. Maybe your English teacher would like to see it."

That evening after everyone was gone and Sue Ellen was in bed, Granny and Uncle Tom also took themselves off. I asked Glen, "Did you and Forrest work something out?"

Glen nodded. "He's really very good with children, isn't he?"

"Yes," I said.

"He told me God had shown him Sue Ellen is like a little oak tree. He said oak trees put down a very deep taproot and once they're rooted, they cannot be dug up and moved. He said he'd have to settle for being Uncle Jay."

Glen paused and then he said, "Forrest said his relationship with Pam had been sin and he had known it clearly at the time. He said sin always has consequences and he has to live with that."

Glen then said hesitantly, "Dria, do you mind if I ask? Do you still think you're in love with him?"

I closed my eyes briefly and opened them again, trying to frame an answer.

Glen said, "You don't have to talk about it."

I sighed. "I had been telling myself it was my imagination, it was just a passing crush, that it would blow over. But today when I saw him, I knew. I love him. I also know he isn't looking at me. And I'll have to live with that."

"Do you want us to help you avoid having to see him?"

"No," I said. "Remember way back before Forrest left, I told you I had been doing some writing and he wanted to help arrange publishing. I passed him a copy of what I've written on a flash drive today and I'm supposed to go out tomorrow morning and talk to him about it. Tomorrow afternoon he's taking Uncle Tom to Springfield to catch his flight home."

When I passed Forrest my flash drive, he had given me a small package. "For later," he said. So up in my room, I opened it but I already knew what was inside. It was the seventh Orphan Arthur book. I opened it up and read the dedication.

> In memory of Ella Hunter, my beloved wife
> who illustrated these books
> and our amazing son, Little Jay Hunter, who inspired them.
> "The Lord gave and the Lord hath taken away;
> blessed be the name of the Lord."
> Job 1:27b

I thought about the story of Job, the righteous man whom God had allowed Satan to test. Forrest's choice of scripture was highly significant. Clearly he had come to terms with the deaths of Ella and Little Jay and had regained his faith in God.

I started reading the book and was enthralled. I could not stop until I came to the end at 3 o'clock in the morning. It would be the last book in the series. In it, the old king died and the wicked witch almost got George and Georgana. But Arthur valiantly protected them and after many hardships, brought them successfully to the Kingdom's cathedral at the time George should be crowned king.

But it was not George who was crowned king. It was Arthur.

The wise old priest explained to Arthur how they had not wanted the next king of Woodsdale to be brought up as a spoiled brat, using his rank and privileged birth to get his way. They had wanted him to grow up patient and brave, able to endure difficulties, and understanding it was his job to protect the weak and defenseless. So they had placed him as protector to the slow-minded twins and he had shown his true character by his constant care and diligent defense of the changelings.

When I finished the book, I started praying. I had asked God to take away how I felt about Forrest so many times, I decided it was useless to keep asking. Instead I asked God for strength to live with loving him when he didn't love me.

Chapter 19: Dragon Hold

The next morning, I didn't start out to Forrest's until after 9 o'clock. I had been busy but truthfully, most of it could have been left for someone else to do. I knew I was nervous about talking to Forrest alone. I would not be alone in the house with him. He had said casually, "Come tomorrow morning. My housekeeper will be there."

When I buzzed from the gate, no one spoke to me. The gate just opened and I drove in. I saw the sign "Dragon Hold" and thought again about Forrest being rather like a dragon. But then I remembered my thoughts about Pam and decided maybe I also was a dragon. Gloria's mother met me at the door and said, "Go on up. He's expecting you."

Forrest was seated at his desk and I could see he had my book open on his computer. He swiveled his chair around and motioned me into my usual seat. "It's great," he said. "You've done a marvelous job with editing and formatting. I've been all the way through and only caught one small error."

I said, "That's good." Then I asked, "Do you think I should change the name of the main character? I chose it long ago but now there's Mary Ruth and Sue Ellen. I wondered if their parents would object."

Forrest grinned and said, "The girls will love it."

I said, "I read your book last night. I couldn't stop reading. I was up half the night. It's great."

He looked at me and smiled and my heart almost stopped. He said, "Dria, how have you been?"

I nodded. "Fine. I like living here with Granny Davis."

"Are you and Glen getting married?"

It was so direct. Maybe that's why I gave a direct answer, "No."

"Glen is a good man, a good father, and he says you love Sue Ellen, so why not?" he asked.

"Because I'm in love with you."

I saw his face go blank. I said, "Forrest, it's okay. You don't have to do anything about it. It's just how it is. I love you but you don't love me. I will just have to live with it."

He got up out of his chair and walked over to the glass doors which open on to a balcony. He was running his hand through his hair like he always did when agitated and he was muttering something to himself.

I tried again. "Forrest, it really is okay."

He turned and looked at me and said, "Dria, I'm not a good person to fall in love with. Sometimes I'm even violent."

"Are you?" I challenged him.

He turned and looked out over the trees, running his hand through his hair again. Then he turned to me and said, "When I paid Pam off, I warned her if she ever showed up here again, I had an unmarked grave waiting for her. I meant it."

I nodded. "And I decided if it looked like she was getting Sue Ellen again, I was going to give her an unmarked grave. I even planned where and how . . . and what I was going to do to cover it up."

"Dria?" He was looking at me in shock. "Why?"

"Sue Ellen told me something. Glen caught Pam once making inappropriate pictures of Sue Ellen naked so he explained to Sue Ellen where no one was supposed to touch her. It was a good thing he did because Ray tried." I saw Forrest turning pale and I said, "Sue Ellen told him to stop and Pam told him Sue Ellen would tell Glen so nothing actually happened. When I told Glen what Sue Ellen told me he said he was going to kill Ray. I said if he did that, he'd end up in jail and what would happen to Sue Ellen? I've had time to think it all over. When Pam and Ray were arrested, they were high on cocaine. If Pam ever got Sue Ellen back, she would end up being badly abused. If Glen or you either one killed Pam, everyone would suspect. But if I do it, no one will really suspect me."

Forrest was looking at me in total disbelief. He finally said, "I can't believe it."

I thought what I had said scared him. I said, "I'm sorry, Forrest. You don't know me all that well. I'm young but I'm learning. Sometimes a person needs to just take action."

He shook his head. "You're like your little Mary Ellen. When something was wrong, she went after it."

"Yes," I said.

Forrest had stopped pacing and running his hand through this hair. He stood still, facing me, looking me full in the face. He said, "Dria, I love you."

I thought about it. "Are you sure?" I asked.

"Yes," he said.

"But why?" I protested.

He smiled. "The first time I saw you, you were telling Ray that Glen did not beat Pam. When I asked you about it, as you answered, I knew you were telling the truth. When Ray and I left, he said Glen already had himself another woman but from what you said, I thought you were one of Glen's cousins. Then after Ray and Pam's escapade, I went to help clean up and you were never there. When I finally found you there, I started a discussion with Granny partly just to watch you." He smiled. "I have never had anyone cite the book of Job before. Job isn't popular. No one wants to believe they may have bad things happen to them when they haven't done anything wrong." Forrest stopped and then said, "Dria, you're strong. You're strong inside. You're strong in your faith in God." He paused again and then said, "I think it was your faith, yours and Granny's, that sent me searching for my lost faith."

I looked Forrest in the eyes and quoted Job, " 'Though He slay me, yet will I trust in Him.' "

Forrest nodded. "Tom told me all about your family, about your mother's accident leaving her in a nursing home for years. Then you lost you grandmother in a surgery which should have been routine. Then your father was murdered and the wheels of justice are stuck with his killer still running around loose. But none of this destroyed your faith."

I sighed. "I hadn't thought of it like that. Life happens one day at a time and I think faith does too. When I take things to God, He gives me peace. It's not peace because He takes away the storm. It's peace in spite of the storm. Does that make sense?"

Forrest nodded. "It's not like the storm isn't there. It's like He is there with you in the storm."

I nodded. "Forrest, I'm really happy you've found your faith again."

"Will you marry me?" he asked.

I had not expected the question. I looked at him and I saw love in his eyes. "Okay," I told him. "I will."

He crossed the room and stood in front of me. "May I kiss you?" he asked.

"Yes," I answered. He put his arms around my waist and kissed my lips. It was nice. Then he looked at me and said, "You've never really been kissed before, have you?"

"No," I said.

"Are you really sure you want to marry me?" he asked.

"Yes," I said and I put my arms around his neck and initiated another kiss. He took some time with this one. His hands were stroking my back and I caressed his neck and ran my hands through his hair. I liked it. I liked it a lot.

I felt his hand caressing my bare skin at my waist under my blouse and then it slipped under the waistband of my trousers. I knew from the teaching in my youth group at church that this was crossing a line. I also knew I didn't want to stop. Before I had time to think it through, Forrest removed his arms and gently pushed himself away from me. He said, "Time to stop."

I looked at him in confusion. I don't know what Forrest saw in my face but he asked, "Dria?"

I said, "No wonder so many people get in trouble. Is it always like this?"

"No," he answered smiling. "It does vary some but it's a risky activity. Just now with you, I didn't expect it to get out of hand so quick."

I shook my head. "I had no idea."

He laughed and said, "When and where?"

I thought of his story-making activity with the boys. "As soon as we can arrange it at Green Valley Chapel. We can get Uncle Tom to stay another day or two."

"You don't want a big wedding?"

"No." I answered. "Everyone is here except my friend, Regina. I'll get her a flight ticket. Maybe Justin Schwartz and his wife. It would be nice if they could come."

Forrest nodded and said, "And I'd like it in writing that you keep your money."

I smiled. "Did we tell you about two of your former Marine buddies trying to find you in January? They told us about the patents."

Forrest shook his head. "Nothing stays a secret around here, does it? Financially, I'm secure but you're more than secure. I don't want anyone to think I married you for your money."

"If you really want something, Justin Schwartz can write it up."

"Where do you want to live?" he asked.

"Would you mind if we lived here at Dragon Hold?" I asked.

"Are you sure?" he asked. "Ella and I built this place together. Even if I took down her paintings and changed everything she chose, she is still a part of the fabric of this house."

I nodded. "I know," I told him. "She is also part of who you are. Never try to forget her. Her life meant something and should never be forgotten."

He was quiet, silent and still. I saw tears build in his eyes and one escaped and ran down his cheek. "You understand," he whispered.

I nodded. "We can name our first daughter Ella in her memory."

He turned his head to look at the seventh illustration on his wall. "We wanted more children but when Ella was pregnant with Little Jay, she had serious blood sugar problems and the doctors didn't recommend her having any more children. Ella was a adopted child, like my grandmother. When I went looking for Ella's biological family, I found her mother had committed suicide soon after she was born. I tracked down Ella's father's family and discovered he had died of diabetes before he was thirty." He signed. "I've finally reached the point I can thank God for the time she did have and the blessing she was to me and others."

When he was quiet, I said, "And she will not be forgotten."

He looked at me and asked, "How many small dragons do you want?"

"At least four," I told him. "After that, we can decide if we want more."

He smiled at me and said, "A lot of work, a lot of risk – and a lot of love. We're going to have fun, aren't we?"

"Yes," I promised.

Points to Ponder

1. Do you believe in Second Sight? Premonitions of any kind? How about prophesies from God?

2. What about bad things happening to Christians? Were Job's torments testing that God allowed or was Job guilty of some sin, as some theologians have postulated?

3. What about faith? Job said he would trust God even if He killed him. Was that faith or bragging?

4. What about salvation? Is a statement of belief in Jesus enough to enter Heaven?

5. Is divorce ever justified? If so, under what circumstances? Is the divorced person free to remarry?

6. Is taking the law into your own hands ever justified? If so, under what circumstances?

7. Is a parent justified in having a drug using child forcibly taken to a drug rehabilitation center?

8. If a person repents of sin and is forgiven, does that erase the potential consequences of that sin?

9. What about gun control?

10. What about exposing children to Fairy Tales? Science Fiction stories? Are there limits on what kind of fantasy stories you think they should read or see?

OHP
Ozark Heritage Publishing

ozarkheritagepublishing@gmail.com

Printed by CreateSpace, an Amazon.com company.

Made in the USA
Columbia, SC
18 October 2020